/25

New Sensations

"Hike!" Matt finally shouted, and Eric snapped him the ball. He dropped back and looked for an open receiver.

"Here!" Stacy yelled. "I'm wide open!"

In a burst of speed, Zack dove through the air and engulfed Stacy with both arms in a rugged tackle. They hit the ground together with a terrible thud.

Oh, no! Zack said to himself in anguish.

Slowly, Stacy opened her eyes and met his anxious gaze. Her wide-eyed, innocent look sent a flood of new sensations through Zack.

"I'm fine," Stacy whispered, barely moving her lips. She seemed to be feeling the same tingly way he did.

MEAN TO ME

M.E. Cooper

SCHOLASTIC INC.
New York Toronto London Auckland Sydney

ISBN 0-590-41686-3

12 11 10 9 8 7 6 5 4 3 2 1   8 9/8 0 1 2 3/9

Printed in the U.S.A.   01

First Scholastic printing, June 1988

Chapter
1

Stacy Morrison smoothed another layer of cocoa butter on her already richly tanned arms and shoulders, then squinted up at the blazing Maryland sun. It was June twenty-first — the longest day of the year — and that suited Stacy just fine.

A perfect day for the beach, she thought, lazily stretching her arms above her head. All around her were other members of the crowd from Kennedy High, gathered as usual at their favorite spot. No one really knew when this particular stretch of sand had been designated the crowd's special preserve, but it was as strong a tradition as Senior Skip Day and the end-of-the-year bonfire. Ever since graduation, the gang had spent every free moment there, comparing notes on summer jobs and college plans. They traded ideas about next year at Kennedy High and

1

gossiped about goings-on in Rose Hill, the suburb of Washington D.C. they all called home.

Stacy brushed some sand from the side of her black bathing suit, which was still damp from her recent dip in the ocean. Her light brown hair was pulled back in a French braid so that it would stay out of her face when she swam. She pushed her mirrored sunglasses down on her turned-up nose and rolled over onto her stomach. Propping herself up on her elbows, she grinned at the close-knit group surrounding her.

Off to her left, Jonathan Preston, one of the recently graduated seniors and a longtime student leader at Kennedy, was busy trying to cover his girlfriend, Lily Rorshack, with sand. She, of course, was trying to squirm away. Both of them finally collapsed in giggles, but not before they sprayed sand all over anyone within reach.

"Hey, Preston!" Greg Montgomery yelled, shaking the grit out of his hair. "One more blast of sand out of you, and it's war!" He aimed the bottle of suntan lotion he was holding at Jonathan and threatened to squirt it at him. "Suntan lotion at thirty paces?"

"Oh, no, you don't!" Greg's girlfriend, Katie Crawford, cried, wrestling the slippery bottle out of his hands. "I've got better things for you to do with that!" Greg grinned as he squeezed a line of lotion across Katie's muscular, freckled back.

Meanwhile, Lily took advantage of the diversion to slip away from Jonathan and race away across the sand toward the water. He leaped up in hot pursuit, and soon their shouts of laughter could be heard from the surf.

Stacy still couldn't believe her luck. Since transferring from Stevenson High, which had closed last year, she had been accepted by the group as one of their own, even though she was just a sophomore. The fact that Katie had taken her under her wing and encouraged her, both as a gymnast and as a person, had helped a lot.

Stacy reached up to the necklace dangling around her neck, unconsciously touching the little charm Katie had given her on graduation night. She let out a heavy sigh. Next year, Katie would be away at the University of Florida. Already Stacy knew that she would miss her terribly.

On a blanket to her right was Daniel Tackett, next year's editor of Kennedy's newspaper, *The Red and the Gold*. He was futilely trying to read the Sunday edition of the *Washington Post*, but the brisk sea breeze kept whipping the pages of the paper every which way. A strong burst of wind flipped the editorial section against his face like a fan, and Daniel groaned loudly, shaking his fist at the cloudless sky.

Karen Davis turned up her tortoiseshell sunglasses and, cupping her hands around her mouth, called teasingly, "What's the matter, Tackett? Can't hack it?"

Daniel cast a mock menacing glance in her direction. "I was about to offer to share the latest news with you," he said, his voice a model of wounded dignity, "but if you are going to stoop so low as to make fun of — "

"Okay, okay!" Karen interrupted with a laugh. "Spare me the speech!"

Her boyfriend, Brian Pierson, crawled across

3

the sand with her, and the two of them sprawled on either side of Daniel, holding the pages down with their feet.

Stacy giggled and shook her head. What a wacky group of friends she had hooked up with.

Two figures, as different as night and day, appeared just then over the top of the nearest dune. Matt Jacobs, shirtless, wearing long surfing shorts and Ray-Ban sunglasses, was listening to Eric Shriver, who, in his khaki shorts, crew shirt, and topsiders, looked like an advertisement for L.L. Bean. They burst out laughing and jogged down the dune toward Stacy and the others.

A shadow fell across Stacy's line of vision, and she turned to see who it was. Little goosebumps suddenly crept up her arm. Standing behind her was Zachary McGraw, all-city quarterback and one of the most gorgeous guys at Kennedy High.

"Hey, Zack, aren't you supposed to be at football practice?" Matt Jacobs called.

"Give me a break," Zack replied, breaking into an easy laugh. "Summer vacation is just hitting its stride. Practice won't get started for another month."

"Well, as an avid fan," Eric said, "I'm anxious to see you strut your stuff as the Cardinals' star quarterback."

"We're counting on you, big guy, to take us all the way," Matt added.

"Just what I need," Zack replied, wincing good-naturedly. "A little more pressure."

Like Stacy, Zack was a mid-year transfer from Stevenson. He had yet to play any real football for Kennedy, but his reputation was almost legendary. Stacy was one of the few people at the beach who had seen him play before. In fact, she had gone to every one of his games. Her slowly growing, secret crush had turned her into Zachary McGraw's biggest fan. But something funny always happened to Stacy when Zack was around.

"He's probably lost his touch," she heard herself suddenly saying to Matt and Eric. "Just another flash in the pan."

Stacy couldn't believe what she had just said, only she couldn't help herself. It was almost as if Zack's presence always flipped a switch inside her. Every remark that came out of her mouth about him was a teasing putdown. It was especially strange for Stacy to treat Zack that way, when she was an incorrigible flirt around other guys. All her bad-mouthing kept Zack safely away from her. Maybe Stacy was just afraid of not succeeding in attracting him.

Zack, who had been laughing along with Matt and Eric, turned to Stacy with a confused look. The expression on his face was so perplexed it looked comical, and Stacy jumped on the chance to toss off another barb.

"Is *this* the face of a star quarterback?" Stacy asked the group around her.

As everybody laughed at her antics, a little voice inside her screamed, *Stop this! It's not going to get you anywhere*. But she couldn't stop.

Zack stared at Stacy in stolid silence as the tips of his ears turned red with embarrassment. She could tell her relentless needling was really starting to get to him.

5

"I think we should begin your training right now," Matt said, clapping Zack on the shoulder. "The sooner, the better."

"I'll go for that!" Greg Montgomery chimed in, getting up from the blanket to join them. "But with what?"

Matt fought hard to keep a straight face as he pointed toward Eric. "Luckily, Coach Shriver here remembered to bring the equipment."

With an impish grin, Eric revealed what he had been hiding behind his back — a beat-up leather football that he'd had since the sixth grade. "Hey, Zack, catch!"

He flipped the ball to Zack, who caught it easily with one hand. Zack raised the ball above his head and asked, "Who's up for a game of touch football?"

Stacy wanted to shout out, "Me, I am!" but something about the look Zack had given her moments before stopped her cold. She had half raised her hand, but quickly ran it across her hair.

Most of the boys and a few of the girls jumped up to join Zack, forming a semicircle in the sand. They quickly divided into teams, with Zack captaining one and Matt heading up the other.

Stacy instantly leaped to her feet and skipped over to Matt. "Can I be on your team?" she asked, looking up at him flirtatiously. "I promise not to drop the ball."

Matt laughed, knowing full well how good an athlete Stacy was. "You're on!"

The group headed toward a vacant stretch of beach, and Stacy found herself walking beside

6

Zack. He was wearing a yellow T-shirt, cut off short, revealing his tautly muscled stomach. His nearness made her head spin, and before she knew what she was doing, Stacy reached out and playfully slapped Zack across his bare midriff.

Zack, caught completely by surprise, buckled over, and Stacy crowed, "This game's going to be easy. Mr. Football Star here is really out of shape."

A couple of the guys hooted with laughter. Everyone knew that Zack was a maniac about conditioning, and his incredible body was proof of the long hours he spent at the gym.

Zack stopped for a moment and, trying to maintain his composure, pulled a tube of zinc oxide from the pocket of his shorts. He dabbed another layer on his nose. While he was putting the tube away, Stacy darted in and rubbed it off before he had time to react.

"Hey, cut it out!" Zack said, his temper near the boiling point. He pointed at Stacy and snapped, "Do you want to play football, or what?"

"What's it to you?" Stacy shot back. She looked at him defiantly, a mocking grin on her face, almost daring him to blow up.

She knew Zack still felt like a newcomer to the crowd, and he obviously wasn't eager to make a scene in front of everyone. He took a deep breath and said quietly, "Nobody's forcing you to, that's all."

"I don't really care if I play or not," Stacy retorted.

Zack shrugged and walked past her, tossing the ball in the air. Grinning coyly at Matt and

Eric, Stacy caught it and shrieked, "Last one to the water is a rotten egg!"

Tucking the ball under one arm, she ran for all she was worth up the dune. As she burst over the top and headed down toward the water's edge, she heard footsteps pounding behind her. Stacy prayed they were Zack's.

Roxanne Easton watched the group of kids zoom past her down the beach and tossed her thick, tawny hair defiantly. The crowd at Kennedy High had made it very clear how they felt about her, and for the past few months they had been giving her the big freeze. But Roxanne was nothing if not determined.

She arched her back in a languorous stretch, extending her perfectly proportioned legs out across the sand. Then she peered discreetly through her dark lashes to see if Vince DiMase was watching her. Her hot pink designer suit with its plunging back and French-cut legs displayed her figure beautifully. Vince's look of total admiration confirmed that. Roxanne let out a satisfied sigh and leaned back on her elbows, studying her new boyfriend's profile.

Vince DiMase was tall, dark and handsome — and so naive. When Roxanne had insisted they lay out their towels a short distance away from the group from Kennedy, Vince had assumed it was because Roxanne wanted a little privacy for the two of them. But she knew better.

Vince leaned forward to watch the football game, the taut muscles on his arms and sides standing out as he shifted his weight. Roxanne had to admit that he looked terrific. All the time he spent rock climbing had certainly paid off, and she was relieved to see he'd shed his usual flannel shirt and blue jeans for a simple maroon swimsuit. At least in that, Vince didn't look like such a backwoods clod.

A burst of laughter came from the center of the group, and Roxanne felt a tight knot of envy grip her stomach. Her ex-best friend, Frankie Baker, was laughing at a joke her boyfriend, Josh Ferguson, had made. The thought of Frankie, who had been a nobody back at Stevenson, being more popular than she was, infuriated Rox. She abruptly turned her back on them.

Face it, Roxanne thought sourly, you've got your work cut out for you. This summer she would have to be more subtle, more devious than ever.

Vince was her ticket back into the group. He was devoted to her — she had made sure of that, playing the innocent damsel to his white knight for all it was worth. And Vince was Josh Ferguson's best friend. It was inevitable. They would have to accept her eventually, and then Roxanne would find herself back at the center of things — where she belonged.

As if on cue, Vince reached over and lightly squeezed her hand. She leaned her head gently against his shoulder, pretending to gaze dreamily into his deep brown eyes. His expression was one of such trust and unshielded admiration that a tiny smile crept across her lips. I may be on the outs with the crowd, Rox thought, but I sure haven't lost the Easton touch!

9

* * *

"The XB70 combines the power of a main-frame with the flexibility of a PC. Talk about state of the art!"

Frankie Baker's light eyes sparkled with lively intensity as she gushed on about her passion — computers. "We're talking about megabytes of RAM built right in. . . ." The bewildered looks on her friends' faces made her pause in mid-sentence. Frankie grinned and added simply, "I mean, it does everything!"

"Will it serve you breakfast and drive you to school?" Jonathan Preston cracked from behind his sunglasses. He ducked as Frankie playfully tossed one of her beach thongs at him across their circle of towels.

"Give her twenty minutes with this beast," Josh piped up, "and I bet Frankie'd have a program for that!"

There was a noisy chorus of agreement from the others, and Frankie felt herself blush with pride. It felt good, being liked and accepted by the most ambitious and friendliest kids in Rose Hill.

Looking around at her new friends, she marveled at how quickly things had changed. Six months ago she wouldn't have been able to talk, let alone joke, with the Kennedy "in" crowd. She wouldn't have had the confidence.

Of course, a lot of her newfound strength had come from getting to know Josh. He was lying on his stomach next to her, his sunglasses perched crookedly on top of his wavy dark hair. Suddenly Frankie felt a fierce urge to hug him.

Just as quickly, her face went somber again,

remembering her dilemma. "The problem is," she announced glumly, "the XB70 costs a bundle, and I can't find a job."

"Gee, Frankie, you're such a whiz with programming," Pamela said. "I would think a lot of businesses would want to hire you."

"Yeah, don't temp agencies need programmers?" Brian suggested.

"Temp agencies?" Josh raised up on his elbow indignantly and dropped his sunglasses onto his nose. "Frankie should be working for a major corporation like IBM or Digital."

Frankie grinned and ruffled Josh's hair affectionately. "It's a little hard," she explained, "convincing a big corporation that a lowly junior from Kennedy High is the answer to all their business problems."

"What's this 'junior' stuff?" Daniel Tackett protested with a grin. "We're seniors now, and don't you forget it!"

Frankie hit her head with the heel of her hand. "Right. I just can't get used to it." She repeated the word in an awed whisper. "Senior."

They all were silent, absorbing the magnitude of the word.

"Out with the old, and in with the new," Jonathan added, his voice filled with melancholy. He had just graduated.

Lily couldn't resist teasing him. "That's right, Gramps," she creaked in her best little-old-lady voice, "It's time for you old fogeys to be moseying along, to make room for us young whippersnappers."

"Old fogey?" Jonathan yelped, snapping out

of his blue mood. "Well, this old fogey can show you a thing or two!" With that he lunged across the blanket and tickled Lily in the ribs hard, making her shriek with laughter. She managed to reach around and get him under the arm. Soon the two of them were giggling hysterically and rolling around on the sand.

"Boy, you guys are a lot of help," Pamela shouted over their howls. "Here Frankie is having an employment crisis, and all you can do is try to tickle each other to death."

Jonathan and Lily stopped giggling abruptly, just as a familiar voice wafted through the air.

"You know, Frankie," Roxanne said sweetly, "one of my mother's boyfriends owns the Foxy Lady boutique, a really exclusive dress shop in Georgetown. It sells strictly one-of-a-kind, designer clothing." Roxanne laughed slyly and added, "I mean, you can't buy a *bath*ing suit in there for less than a hundred dollars!"

Just hearing Roxanne's voice made Frankie wince. She'd almost forgotten her ex-friend was with them — which was pretty hard considering that Roxanne usually made herself the center of attention wherever she went.

Frankie watched as Rox glanced around the circle to see if everyone was suitably impressed, then smiled over at her. "Well, my mom convinced George to hire me for the summer. I'm sure she could talk him into giving you a job, too."

There was an awkward silence as Frankie didn't respond but instead looked steadily down at the ground. Roxanne hesitated for just a moment, then pressed on.

"I mean, since you and I have been good friends for so long."

Frankie didn't like being reminded of their soured friendship. Nor did she want all of her new friends to think about it.

"Besides, you know how fond my mother is of you," Roxanne finished.

Frankie fought hard to suppress the bitter laugh that welled up in her throat. Mrs. Easton was so involved in maintaining her image as one of Washington's most popular society hostesses, she rarely gave more than a passing thought to her own children, let alone her children's friends.

Frankie struggled with the mixed emotions churning inside her. She had spent so many years in Roxanne's shadow, letting Rox dominate her ruthlessly. Roxanne had constantly manipulated Frankie into helping her carry out her little schemes and, too often, innocent people had gotten hurt. Frankie had finally rebelled and broken away last spring, and she had never regretted it. She didn't want to get mixed up with Rox again now.

"Uh, no thanks," Frankie replied flatly, deliberately not looking in Roxanne's direction. There was a tense silence as everyone waited to see how Roxanne would respond to the snub.

It was Vince who broke the silence. "Rox's mom is really kind of special, isn't she?" he said, his voice pleasantly husky and warm. "She helped Rox get that job, even after Rox totaled her new

Mercedes. Most parents would have grounded her for the summer, at least — if not for life!"

Everyone laughed, and that relieved the tension. Even Frankie smiled a little. Roxanne, however, had to think quickly.

Torrey, Rox's younger brother, had been recklessly driving Roxanne out to the crowd's private beach party when they got into a serious accident. They told the police and their mother the truth — that underage Torrey had been driving. But then suddenly Vince had driven up in his rescue truck, and Rox had used the accident to her advantage: She told Vince that she had been so upset about their fight that she shouldn't have been driving her mother's Mercedes. The accident was all her fault. Sympathetic Vince totally believed her little story, and took her right back into his arms. But now it seemed as though she'd have to spread the lie a little further.

"Well, Mother knew I wouldn't have had an accident if I hadn't have been so upset," Roxanne explained, her voice contrite and apologetic, yet loud enough that everyone could hear. "Vince and I had a . . . misunderstanding, and I got so distraught that I lost control and drove right off the road!"

Frankie watched Roxanne blink her luminous green eyes adoringly up at Vince. She'd seen Roxanne give guys that look hundreds of times before. It was her patented turn-them-to-mush look, and it always worked. At least, in the beginning.

"I don't know what I would have done if Vince hadn't rescued me." Roxanne added a slight quiver to her sultry voice. Frankie wanted to gag.

"You know, my squad at the volunteer fire-fighters went to a trauma treatment seminar recently," Vince said, looking around at the group. "They told us that it can take weeks, even months for a person to recover from the emotional stress caused by an accident. Even when they're not physically injured themselves."

He leaned in close to Roxanne and murmured, "It must have been so awful for you."

"Oh, I'll be all right," Roxanne replied, and laughed to herself. What a bunch of suckers, she thought, before starting in again. "Something like that's always easier when you have wonderful people around to help you through it." She smiled at Vince, then shook her head slowly. "In a way, I feel so lucky, you know? My mom really has been wonderful." Her voice shook again, as she added, "I've had to think a lot about my mistakes over the past few months. . . ." Roxanne paused to make sure she had everyone's attention. "I think I've really become a better person."

She was pleased to see Matt and Jonathan smiling warmly in her direction. *Good*, she thought with satisfaction, they've been completely taken in. There's nothing like a little drama to soften people up. One small victory for me.

Roxanne opened her mouth to say something else, when a shadow settled on the sand in front of her. With an embarrassed start she realized they weren't smiling at her at all, but at the girl standing behind her.

Chapter
2

"**B**renda Austin!" Jonathan and Pamela shouted simultaneously as a familiar figure clad in baggy twill shorts and a faded green T-shirt walked toward them across the sand.

"Hi, gang!" Brenda called out, waving back merrily. She'd graduated from Kennedy High the previous year and had decided to pay a surprise visit to her old crowd's hangout on the beach. Driving over, the thought had struck her that there might be no one there she knew. After all, a whole year had gone by. But as Brenda watched her old friends running to greet her, she thought to herself, some things never change!

Jonathan reached her first. "Gosh, it's great to see you!" He lifted her up in a big bear hug and swung her around in a circle.

"Wow, what a welcome!" Brenda said as Jonathan set her back down on the sand. "I should come back more often."

"What brings you here, stranger?" he asked.

Before Brenda could reply, Pamela smothered her with a hug and questions of her own. "Brenda, we've missed you! How are you doing? *What* are you doing?"

"One at a time, one at a time!" Brenda held her hands up in front of her.

Jonathan pulled an imaginary zipper across his mouth and gestured for Pamela to do the same. They both stared expectantly at Brenda, their eyes twinkling.

Brenda hesitated, then burst out laughing. "Now I don't know where to start."

"Well, come on and sit down," Jonathan said. "I'll introduce you to all these new faces."

There was more merriment as he led Brenda over to their circle of friends. Brian, Karen, Greg, Eric, and the rest of Brenda's old friends added their warm greetings.

"So how does it feel to have finished your first year at Georgetown?" Brian asked pleasantly. Then he groaned. "I'm certainly not looking forward to being a freshman all over again."

"To tell you the truth," Brenda admitted with a grin, "I've been so busy with my psychology classes, I haven't had time to feel like a frosh at all."

"Are you still working at Garfield House?" Pamela asked. Garfield was a halfway house for runaway teens located near the university.

Brenda nodded. "I'm counseling runaways there part-time." She beamed with pride. "It's great! I get to do the kind of work I'm interested in, and I get paid for it, too!"

The conversation rippled around the group as they all, particularly the just-graduated seniors, pumped Brenda for more of her impressions of college life. As she talked, Brenda looked around the circle of eager faces, all hanging on her every word, and thought to herself, You've come a long way, baby!

Two years ago, Brenda Austin would never have found the nerve to speak so confidently in front of other people, especially when she'd never met some of them before. Of course, two years ago she had been a runaway at Garfield house herself, a textbook definition of a troubled teen. Full of anger at her mother for remarrying, and jealous of her overachieving stepsister Chris, she had been consumed with guilt about her feelings, but unable to resolve them. Her frustration and helplessness had made her feel like hiding away from the world.

The counselors at Garfield House had helped her get a handle on her problems. And she slowly began making friends at Kennedy, which also helped. But best of all, she finally became close to Chris. That was the icing on the cake.

"Hey, we should have a big get-together," Jonathan piped up.

"Still the same old Jonathan," Brenda commented with a laugh. "Kennedy High's resident cruise director!"

"Sounds like fun," Lily chimed in. "Let's decide when."

"Actually, guys, I've got a better idea," Brenda broke in. She waited until she had everyone's attention, then said, "The real reason I came out here today was to ask you all a favor." She glanced over at Frankie and the other new kids and repeated, "Everyone included. You guys know about the big Fourth of July parade in Georgetown. It's pretty neat — lots of marching bands and floats. . . ."

There were scattered nods around the crowd, and Brian said, "Yeah, it's supposed to be one of the best parades anywhere."

"Well, the kids at Garfield House want to create a crazy float for the parade, but they can't do it alone." Brenda lowered her voice to sound like a marine corps recruiter. "We're looking for a few fun people to help us come up with a really wild and wacky entry. Anyone you know fit that description?"

Jonathan turned to his friends and somberly asked, "Will all those present who have a keen and scientific interest in designing a wild and wacky float please raise your *right* hand?"

Everyone raised his or her left hand and turned, straight-faced, to Brenda, who burst out laughing.

"I take it that means you'll help?" she asked with a grin.

"Absolutely!" Josh exclaimed. "It'll be a blast."

"Hey, lots of people from the old gang are back in town for the summer," Jonathan announced. "Maybe we can rope them into this."

"Like who?" Brenda asked quickly. Even though they had gone their separate ways, she was always curious to hear about her old friends.

"Well, Ted and Brad both called me just last week," Jonathan replied.

At the mention of Brad's name, Brenda smiled warmly. They had been through so much together. It really would be nice to see him again. "Great!" she said. "The more the merrier!"

"Hey, every good parade entry needs music," Brian declared in his best DJ voice. "I could work up a tape for us to use."

"Why not form a band ourselves?" Karen suggested.

"But what about instruments?" ever-logical Frankie asked.

Before Karen could reply, Lily was on her feet, squealing, "I know, trash can lids! We could use them as cymbals!"

"And decorate them ourselves," Pamela added, quickly making a mental inventory of the paint supplies in her art studio at home. "Oooh, and I could paint a big banner to drape across the float! Like the ones I did last year for Homecoming!"

"I could probably get my dad to donate a bunch of those bizarre-looking disposable paper overalls from his factory," Josh announced. "Then our New Wave band can have uniforms."

"And Lily and I will work up some choreographed steps for the marchers," Jonathan exclaimed, springing to his feet.

"Yeah, some real precision moves!" Lily said, giggling as she duck-walked over to his side. "We could do intricate maneuvers like, 'Parade Rest!'" With that they both fell flat on their backs onto the sand.

Their enthusiasm was infectious, and within minutes everyone was shouting out wackier and wackier ideas.

Roxanne felt her chest tighten with frustration. With each passing second, she could see herself being more excluded from what was sure to be the big event of the summer. She had been so patient, waiting for a chance to ease her way back into the group — and now this Brenda Austin had walked in and stolen her thunder. Her mind went into overdrive and suddenly she sprang to her feet.

"I'll make red, white, and blue sashes for our uniforms, with scraps of material from the Foxy Lady," she announced. "They'll add just the right patriotic touch to the entry."

There was a stunned silence as everyone turned to stare at her. No one had even considered including Roxanne in their float plans — particularily Jonathan, Karen, and Brian. Brenda, who didn't even *know* Roxanne, surveyed the scene curiously. As for Frankie, she couldn't believe Roxanne had the gall to try and horn in where she obviously wasn't wanted. She had to bite her tongue to keep from repeating sarcastically, "*Our* uniforms?"

Roxanne ignored the wall of icy glares leveled at her and forged ahead. "Our band will have the first designer uniforms in the history of the Fourth of July!" she enthused.

The awkward stillness hung in the air. No one knew what to say. Finally Vince came to her rescue. "I think that's a wonderful idea, Rox." He looked to his best friend for support. "Don't you think so, Josh?"

Josh felt like he'd been pinned to the hot seat. He didn't want to make Vince look like an idiot by protesting against his girlfriend's idea. Finally he managed to force out a vague nod and a pinched smile in reply.

The others looked at each other uncomfortably, but no one offered any objections to Roxanne's suggestion.

With a great sigh, Roxanne rolled over onto her back on her blanket and stared up into the clear blue sky above. It was decided — she would be included in the crowd's entry to the Fourth of July parade.

She smiled smugly to herself and thought, Score one for me.

"Hey! Zack the Hack!"

Stacy cupped her hands around her mouth and shouted at the muscular blond athlete facing her across the scrimmage line. Her team had possession of the ball and was just a few yards from a touchdown. "We're going to walk all over your face, Zack-O!"

Zack felt his jaw clench involuntarily. He had to remind himself that this was just a dumb touch football game on the beach. Usually Zack could control his temper no matter what, but something about this girl Stacy was really getting on his nerves. She had been on his case the entire game, making wisecracks every time he caught the ball or made a play. He had just about had it with her constant needling.

He shook his head and took a deep breath. As he crouched down on the line of scrimmage, he looked up and down the line of the opposing team. Matt Jacobs, who was acting as quarterback for the "Sharks," as they'd decided to call themselves, was barking out his signals.

"Hike!" Matt finally shouted, and Eric snapped him the ball. He dropped back and looked down the beach for an open receiver.

Everyone was going in all directions. Stacy ran straight across the goal line toward Zack, who backpedaled to keep up with her. Then she stopped dead and turned to face Matt.

"Here," Stacy yelled. "I'm wide open!" Matt arched back and spiraled a pass over Daniel Tackett's head, straight toward Stacy's outstretched arms. If she caught it, the Sharks would win.

Something suddenly clicked in Zack's head. He completely ignored the rules of touch football and, in a burst of speed, dove through the air and engulfed Stacy with both arms in a rugged, bone-crunching tackle. The ball flew past the tips of her outstretched fingers, and they hit the ground together with a terrible thud.

Stacy lay very still, not moving at all. A succession of horrible images flashed through Zack's mind. What if he'd really hurt her? All the school needed was another tragedy like Katie's skiing accident. Stacy might have suffered a concussion, or a broken collarbone!

Oh, no! Zack said to himself in anguish, I just crippled the best and brightest hope of the Kennedy gymnastics team, and all because I don't know how to control my stupid temper!

Zack's arms were still wrapped tightly around Stacy, but he was afraid to move for fear he'd aggravate her injuries.

Slowly, Stacy opened her big blue eyes and met his anxious gaze. Her wide-eyed, innocent look sent a flood of new sensations through Zack.

Suddenly he was acutely aware of the touch of her shoulder, how warm her skin felt against his own, her hair brushing like cornsilk across his neck, the intoxicating realization that she was wearing perfume.

"Are, uh, are you all right?" Zack managed to stammer weakly.

"I'm fine," Stacy whispered, barely moving her lips. She seemed to be feeling the same tingly way he did.

Zack cleared his throat awkwardly. "I was afraid I'd hurt you and ruined your future on the gymnastics team." He noticed the fine layer of freckles sprinkled across her up turned nose, and almost forgot what he was saying. "Anyway . . . I know how important that must be to you."

"Gymnastics is no big deal," she bluffed, her voice a little breathless.

Zack felt totally confused. Moments ago he'd been so angry and frustrated because of this mystifying girl in his arms. Now he wanted nothing more than to kiss her. He leaned gently forward and Stacy dreamily closed her eyes, waiting for the thrill of his lips on hers.

"Hey, Stace!" a loud voice called, ruining the moment. It was Matt, but he seemed to be far, far away. Stacy rolled to one side and quickly sat up.

The game had broken up, and everyone was gathering their things to go home. Matt was shouting over his shoulder as he folded up an old army blanket.

"Hey, Stacy!" Matt repeated. "Everybody's meeting at the sub shop on Friday night. You going to be there or what?"

Stacy shook her head, as if to clear her senses. Zack could tell she still felt a little groggy from the tackle. She turned and looked directly at him.

"Will you be there Friday?" she asked, her voice small and hesitant.

"Will you?" he whispered back. He reached up to brush some sand out of her hair; its silkiness made him dizzy.

"Maybe," Stacy replied, the impish twinkle returning to her voice.

"Then maybe I'll be there, too," Zack replied, a slow grin forming on his face.

"Hey, Morrison, let's go!" The sound of Eric's voice brought them both back down to earth. "The bus to Rose Hill is scheduled to depart in exactly two minutes!"

"Whoops! Can't miss my ride." Stacy scrambled to her feet and, as she edged over the top of the dune, paused just long enough to grin back over her shoulder at Zack.

He watched her disappear, still enjoying the fresh memory of what had happened between them. Then, abruptly, he stopped himself.

Whoa! he ordered himself. Just one minute. Zack shook his head and leaped to his feet. What was he doing? Falling for another girl, that's what! He put his hands on his hips and stared out at the ocean, trying to sort out the maze of feelings that

25

had just swept over him like one of those big swells racing into shore.

Let's face it, he thought glumly. This really isn't my year for romance.

He'd already made a fool out of himself twice. Shortly after arriving at Kennedy, he'd fallen for Holly Daniels, whom he later discovered already had a boyfriend who was away at college. Even more humiliating had been his discovery that Frankie Baker had had a crush on him for years. And by the time he had realized he liked her, too, she had met and fallen in love with Josh. Even now, the memory made him wince.

Then the image of Stacy, the wind rustling her short bangs, looking wide-eyed up into his face, filled his mind. For just a second, he felt his resolve melting away.

Just as quickly he dismissed the thought from his mind. He wasn't about to make the same mistake a third time. He had to look at this rationally. A pretty, fun-loving girl like Stacy wasn't likely to be unattached. Besides, from the way she'd been ribbing him all afternoon, it was obvious that Stacy Morrison thought he was just a big, dumb jock. What had happened between them had to be an act, probabaly one she'd put on just to tease him. Zack knew he wasn't the smartest guy in the world, but he was smart enough to know when he was being taken for a ride.

"It's time to drop back and punt!" he muttered. Turning his back on the ocean, he walked resolutely up the beach toward his car.

Chapter
3

It was Monday afternoon. Frankie Baker skimmed her slender fingers across the shiny keyboard of the glistening new XB70 computer and sighed. The floor model was nestled invitingly in a demonstration carrel near the front door of The Wizard, the best computer store in the Rose Hill Mall. She looked up from the color monitor just in time to catch Josh grinning at her, his eyes bright with affection.

"What's so funny?" she demanded good-naturedly. "Was my mouth hanging open or something?"

Josh shook his head. "I just get a kick out of watching you. It's still amazing to me that a human being could get so much pleasure out of a jumble of microchips."

"Oh, Josh, if you only knew!" Frankie replied wistfully. Then a smile crept over her face, and she nimbly tapped a short program into the computer. The printer buzzed loudly, then proceeded to print something out on a sheet of paper.

"What's going on?" Josh asked, leaning over to watch the progress of the printer.

"You'll see," Frankie replied. Suddenly she felt a little shy when the printer stopped, Josh pulled the paper away from the carriage and examined it curiously. Then his face broke into a wide grin.

"You're something else," he rumbled affectionately, holding the printout up in front of him. Frankie beamed with pleasure. A large heart filled the paper from margin to margin, but a closer look revealed that the pattern had been created by countless repetitions of the name "Frankie." At the center of the heart was the outline of a box. Inside, surrounded by Xs and Os, and in bold print for emphasis, was the name "Josh."

"Incredible," Josh added, "how it can do that so fast."

"This computer's just as great as I remembered it," Frankie agreed. Then her lower lip began to tremble and she blurted, "And I'll never have it! That's all there is to it!" With one angry stroke, she erased the program, spun on her heels, and walked out of the store.

"Whoa, wait a minute!" Josh ran out into the mall after Frankie and led her to a nearby bench. "What kind of talk is that?" he asked, wrapping his arm around her shoulder and giving her a hug. "Come on! We've only begun the job hunt. There are at least ten more stores in the mall that we haven't hit yet."

Frankie leaned heavily against the back of the bench. She reached into her straw tote bag and pulled out a spiral notebook, flipping to the pages she had set aside to keep track of her job search. In neat, precise handwriting were printed all the names of the stores located at the Rose Hill Mall. Across from each name were three columns, in which Frankie listed whom she had contacted at the store, the date and time, and the response.

The response column was depressing, to say the least. Each line said, "already hired summer help" or "too young" or "no experience." Like monotonous variations on a theme, each store manager had given her basically the same reply: "Thanks, but no thanks."

Josh reread the list along with Frankie, and the hopelessness of the situation started to weigh down on his mood. He took a deep breath, grabbed Frankie by the hand, and said, "We need to take time to regroup — *now!* And I know the perfect place."

Before Frankie could protest, she found herself being propelled straight across the mall toward a little shop with a bright yellow awning over the entrance, a huge neon sign in the shape of an ice cream cone, and fancy lettering that read, "The Big Dipper."

Five minutes later they were grinning at each other across two gigantic Banana Fudge Ripple Delights, oozing extra whipped cream and liberally sprinkled with toasted almonds.

With each luscious bite, Frankie felt her sagging spirits revive. She could never stay down for long when Josh was with her. Just being around him made her feel more confident and even prettier. She smiled to herself as she remembered Josh's reaction to her that morning when he'd arrived to pick her up, eager to begin the big job search.

Frankie had already been up for hours, plaiting her long, pale blonde hair into a single French braid down her back. She had chosen a pale pink silk blouse with matching jabot and a navy blue straight linen skirt that hugged her petite figure. White stockings and blue flats completed the picture.

"Oh! I'm sorry!" Josh had stammered, backing away from her front door when she'd opened it. "I must have the wrong house."

Frankie was completely taken by surprise and, thinking that something was wrong with her outfit, stepped back in to check herself in the hall mirror. She looked up to see Josh standing behind her.

"You see, I was looking for Frankie the Kid," he drawled, a lopsided grin on his face. "Used to be the soda fountain girl in a small town. Kind of shy, a little unsure of herself — you know the type." He took her by the shoulders and turned her gently around to face him. "Instead, I think I've found Ms. Frances Baker, young professional — a woman on the move!"

Frankie had hoped she looked grown-up, and Josh's response was a big boost. She had wrapped her arms around him in a big, tight hug.

"Hey, anybody home?"

Frankie jerked herself out of her reverie to see Josh waving his hand in front of her eyes. She sat up straight and reached for her spoon, digging down deep into her rapidly melting sundae.

"Sorry, Josh," she said, feeling a little embarrassed. "What were you saying?"

"What I said was," he repeated slowly, "I know how depressing this job hunt has been. I also know how much you want that computer. So. . . ." This time it was his turn to blush. Josh stared down at his ice cream and, without looking directly at her, asked, "So . . . why don't you accept Roxanne's offer?"

For a second, Frankie thought she had misunderstood him. Then, very carefully, she set her spoon down on the little glass tabletop and stared at Josh, totally appalled. "You know how I feel about her," Frankie said, her voice choked and strained. "How could you, of all people, even suggest that? I couldn't do it!"

Just thinking about Roxanne made Frankie flash back to those awful years of being under Rox's thumb. She thought of all the times she had been humiliated by her supposed best friend. Frankie shuddered. "I just couldn't do it!"

"Frankie, I know you've had some rough times with Roxanne," Josh said, his voice almost a whisper, "but you were different then. You let her walk all over you."

"Yeah," Frankie muttered, "Wearing her highest heels!"

"What I'm saying is," Josh continued, "you're different now. You'd never let that happen and — " He took a deep breath and pushed away his sundae. "The bottom line is, if you really want that computer, this is a way to get it."

"Why are you pushing this?" Frankie demanded. "It's not just me that she's offended.

Look at the way she's treated everyone else! I'm not the only one who mistrusts her — "

"I know, I know," Josh interrupted, holding his hands up in defeat. He looked down at the table for a moment, obviously struggling with some inner conflict. Finally he blurted out, "It's just that . . . well, Vince asked me to talk to you about it. He really thinks she's changed; genuinely. And it's kind of frustrating to him that our friends won't accept Rox at all, won't even give her a chance to prove that she's any different."

Frankie couldn't help rolling her eyes in disbelief. But she also felt her body relax a little. It was a big relief to know that this wasn't Josh's idea.

"I'm pretty skeptical, too," Josh added. "But doesn't Roxanne at least deserve a chance? I mean, the car wreck was an awful experience for anyone to go through, but maybe she learned from it. Vince says now that she's with him, she's not the person she used to be."

"Then Vince is being a big fool! He doesn't know Roxanne like I do," Frankie retorted. "I've known her for *years*. She's just using him to get. . . ." Something about the look in Josh's eyes made her bite her tongue. A horrible silence fell between them, and Frankie stared miserably down at her empty dish.

"I know how you feel about Roxanne," Josh finally said in a quiet, controlled voice. "But Vince is my best friend. My oldest, closest friend. We've known each other since the second grade." He paused and cleared his throat. "And Vince would not — *could* not fall for a girl who didn't have something good about her."

Touched by the anguish in Josh's voice, Frankie lifted her head to look at him.

"Even if he's making a mistake with her," Josh said, "I've got to stick by him."

He looked really sad, and she realized that Josh was horribly torn between his love for her and his loyalty toward his best friend. Impulsively, she leaned forward and kissed him lightly on the cheek. He looked up at her, a little surprised, and she whispered, "You're a good friend. Vince is lucky."

He smiled back at her, a little unsure of what to say. Frankie stared out across the mall, trying to sort out her thoughts. From where they sat, she could see into the window of the computer store. There, blinking at her, was the green monitor of her XB70. The flickering light tugged at her heart. She realized she wanted it, wanted it desperately, more than anything she had ever wanted before in her life. She knew suddenly that she could endure almost anything to get it.

Josh is right, she thought to herself. I am different — more confident, more mature . . . *different*. Frankie smiled. She would never let Roxanne push her around the way she had before. And she had to admit, their relationship hadn't been all bad. Rox had been fun, at times — and maybe she really *had* changed. Like Josh had said, didn't she owe her former friend at least one more chance to prove herself?

Her mind made up, Frankie turned back to Josh, who was quietly, solemnly studying her face.

With one more covetous glance at the computer, Frankie announced, "I'll do it!"

Josh leaned recklessly across the table and, cradling her face in his hands, kissed her. Then he whispered in her ear, "Atta girl!"

Chapter
4

Roxanne Easton sank deeply into the plush cushions of the living room sofa and lazily checked the Le Clip watch attached to her sleeve. Seven o'clock. Only one more hour to endure until her "big" date with Vince. Not that she was all that excited by the prospect, but it *was* Friday night and being with Vince would at least get her out of the house and away from *him*.

The *him* in question was her brother, Torrey, who was slouched in an overstuffed chair across the room. A bored look on his handsome face, the younger Easton stared fixedly at the MTV video blasting from the wide-screen stereo TV their mother had recently purchased. Torrey was wearing his usual uniform — dirty Reeboks with mismatched laces, tight black jeans, and a ripped-up Billy Idol T-shirt. He looked particularly out of place among the sleek furnishings of Mrs. Easton's town house, on which her exclusive

Georgetown decorator had spared no expense.

"Torrey, get your filthy shoes off the coffee table," Roxanne demanded. "You'll scratch the glass and ruin it!"

Without glancing at her, Torrey shifted his weight and pointedly left his feet exactly where they were. Before Roxanne could scold her brother again, a new, deeper voice barked from the doorway.

"Get them off. Now!"

A startled Torrey jumped at the command and dropped his feet to the carpet before he could think about it. Then his eyes blazed, and he stared fiercely at the well-dressed man standing near the door.

The man returned the boy's angry stare and waited, nonchalantly adjusting his cufflinks. Torrey backed down first and turned his attention back to the television. Roxanne couldn't help but smile at her brother's humiliation.

George Royce smoothed the lapels of his silk Armani suit and shook his head in disgust. He had been waiting in the hall for Jodi Easton to finish getting ready for their dinner date but overheard Roxanne chastise her brother. He had only been dating their mother for a few weeks, but already Rox could tell he thought she and Torrey were spoiled rotten. And he seemed quite prepared to do something about it.

The air was suddenly filled with the rich scent of Chanel No. 5, and seconds later Jodi Easton wafted into the room. "George, darling, I need your advice desperately," Mrs. Easton purred, looking spectacular in her strapless summer gown.

The gauzy material was covered with a delicate floral print in olive, mauve, and pale yellow. "Which should I wear, the gold or the pearls?"

She held one necklace than another across her throat, waiting for his advice. Roxanne felt a twinge of jealousy. Why didn't her mother ever ask her? It was obvious that the gold choker was far more appropriate. It glistened against her mother's perfectly bronzed skin and added a warm elegance the pearls couldn't match. But as far as Jodi Easton was concerned, there was no one else in the room but George Royce, who studied her with an admiring eye. Finally he declared, "I think the gold looks best."

Roxanne's mother spun to study her reflection in the gilded mirror above the white marble mantel. "You're right, as usual. Your taste is always exquisite." She turned back around, touched George lightly on the cheek, and floated out of the room.

Roxanne watched her mother's performance in cynical silence. She had witnessed her act dozens of times before. Her mother was an expert in the art of making a man feel needed. Of course, she had planned to wear the gold necklace all along, but by letting George appear to decide, she had skillfully flattered his ego and made him feel important. It was not for nothing that Jodi Easton had earned the reputation of being one of Washington's most courted and popular socialites — and she had certainly worked hard enough to earn the title.

Usually Roxanne felt proud of her mother's position. She often used some of her mother's tricks herself because they worked so well. But tonight Roxanne had a bitter taste in her mouth. The whole time her mother had been in the room, she hadn't so much as glanced at her children. In fact, Mrs. Easton hadn't even acknowledged Roxanne's presence since George's arrival. It wouldn't hurt if her mother spent a little less time worrying about herself, and thought about her children once in a while.

Angrily, Roxanne reached for the remote control on the glass table in front of her and abruptly changed the channel.

"Hey, I was watching that!" Torrey protested, raising up on one elbow.

"So?" Roxanne challenged. "Maybe I wanted to watch something else."

Before Torrey could reply, George interrupted. "So, Roxanne, how do you like working at the Foxy Lady?"

Roxanne glanced up at her mother's boyfriend. George owned several stores in the Washington area and kept a firm watch over all of them. Roxanne shrugged halfheartedly. "It's okay."

As work goes, she wanted to add. If she had her way, Roxanne wouldn't work at all. Then she would have more time to figure out a way for getting back into the crowd at Kennedy High. Suddenly she remembered the Fourth of July Parade and the sashes she had promised to supply, and quickly changed her tactics.

"Oh, George, by the way," Roxanne began, in her sweetest voice, "some of the kids from school are making an entry for the Fourth of July Parade in Georgetown. I told them that you might let us use some of the leftover fabric at the store to make sashes." She looked up at him and asked shyly, "Would that be okay?"

George was clearly surprised by her abrupt change in attitude. "I . . . I don't know, I'll have to think about it. This is a summer project related to your school, is it?"

Roxanne nodded her head. "We're helping put together an entry for Garfield House — you know, the counseling center for runaways." She added pointedly, "I thought the store might want to be associated with a community service project like this."

George nodded appreciatively. "That's very good of you, Roxanne. Of course I'd like to support such a worthwhile cause. When would you make these, uh . . . sashes, did you say?"

"I'd put them together the morning of the parade. The store would already be closed for the holiday so I wouldn't bother anyone at all."

"You'd have to use only the remnants," George instructed. "And I'd hold you personally responsible for cleaning up any mess."

"We'll be very careful," she assured him.

"Well. . . ." George thought quietly for a moment. "Okay, then."

"Thanks, George," Roxanne said, expecting him to now leave the room and join her mother. Instead she watched with dread as George moved toward the couch and sat down beside her.

"By the way, Roxanne," he began, "how does your friend, Frances, like her new job?"

Having got what she wanted, Roxanne had no desire to get chummy with her mother's boyfriend. "I don't know," she muttered. "Why don't you ask her?"

Roxanne reached for the remote control again, but George snatched it out of her hand and switched off the large television completely.

"Hey!" Torrey started to protest but was silenced by a cutting glare from George. Torrey was in enough trouble because of the car accident without adding *more* strikes against himself. George finally turned his attention back to Roxanne. He was quiet for a moment, obviously trying to calm his temper.

She met his gaze with an angry flash of her green eyes but remained silent. The only thing moving on his face was a little muscle that twitched along his jaw.

"Let me point out a few things, young lady," George said finally, his voice measured and controlled. "As an employee of mine, it is your responsibility to take an interest in your work; to care about the quality of our product and be proud of what you are selling. This pride translates itself to the public. On your advice, Roxanne, I hired your friend, Frances — "

"Her name is *Frankie*," Roxanne interrupted defiantly.

The muscle in George Royce's jaw twitched furiously for a moment, then slowly relaxed.

"As a favor to you and your mother, I hired your friend . . . *Frankie*," he said. "As I see it, you are personally responsible for the quality of Frances's — Frankie's — work. That's how a successful business operates."

"Look, I don't need any lectures from you!"

Roxanne burst out, angrily leaping to her feet and storming away from him to the bookcase. "You're not my father! You have no right ordering me around all the time."

"Well, *some*one needs to give the orders around here," George barked back at her, finally letting his temper go. "You kids just run wild. You have no respect for anyone or anything, least of all your — "

Jodi Easton chose that moment to sweep back into the room, and they all fell into an embarrassed silence. "George, darling," she said quietly, looking from him to her children, "is there a problem?"

"There certainly is," George replied evenly. "And her name is Roxanne."

Roxanne stared back at him defiantly.

"Well, whatever it is, let's not let a little misunderstanding ruin our plans for the evening," Mrs. Easton said soothingly. "I was so looking forward to a delightful dinner with you, George."

George hesitated for a moment, then shrugged. "Perhaps you're right. This isn't the time." He stepped quickly out of the room into the hall.

Roxanne could hardly stop herself from laughing out loud. She'd won! For once, her mother had taken her side.

"We should go, or we'll be late for our reservation," Mrs. Easton observed. "Roxanne, what are your plans for the evening?"

"Vince is taking me out," Roxanne replied, still reveling in her victory over George. "We're going to hang out down at the sub shop with the crowd from Kennedy."

"Oh," Jodi Easton commented vaguely. "Well, have a good time. And Torrey, try to keep yourself occupied while you're here alone tonight." She blew them kisses, which they both ignored, and turned to go through the door into the hall, only to find her way blocked by George.

"I'm sorry, Jodi, I can't let it slide," he said briefly. George focused his attention on Roxanne and said, "I find it simply incomprehensible that this insolent daughter of yours can be responsible for wrecking your brand-new Mercedes and not be punished for it. Torrey's been placed on restriction, hasn't he? I suppose it won't do *him* much good, though."

"Now, George," Mrs. Easton purred, trying to calm him down, "we've been through all that before."

"I'm serious, Jodi," he responded. "Believe me, I understand how difficult it is for a single mother to raise two children alone." As Mrs. Easton started to protest, George cut her off. "I don't mean to criticize, but I think it's very important that some discipline be imposed, and I think tonight is a good time to start."

"What do you suggest?" Mrs. Easton asked, a little taken aback.

"I think Roxanne should be grounded, too," he said flatly. "Indefinitely."

"What!" Roxanne exploded from across the room. "Mother! You can't let him do that. He has no right!"

Mrs. Easton looked confused, unsure of what to do, and Roxanne's spirits sank. "Don't you think you're being a bit severe, George?" she said

42

cautiously. "I mean, it is a bit after the fact for punishment."

"For the weekend, then," George muttered grimly. "That really isn't enough to make up for wrecking the car, but at least it's a start."

"Y-you can't do this to me!" Roxanne spluttered. "*I* wasn't driving! And how will this look in front of my friends? I'll look like a complete idiot!"

Mrs. Easton looked at her, then uncertainly back at George. "Perhaps George is right," she said finally. "Perhaps I haven't done the right thing."

"Mother!" Roxanne screamed. "You can't side with him. You can't!"

"I'm sorry, dear," her mother said. "George is right. You need to learn to take responsibility for your actions."

Just then Roxanne saw her brother squirming in his seat, his back to George, practically convulsed with laughter. Torrey had been given a ticket and several strikes against his impending license, but that was nothing for Torrey; he was used to being in trouble. Roxanne, however, had gotten off easily with the accident. Because she wasn't driving, Roxanne was in much less trouble than her brother was. But Torrey held a trump card over Rox's head: He knew that she'd lied to Vince, and there was always the threat that Torrey would squeal.

As she spun around to face him, there was a loud ring and Torrey said, "Saved by the bell. Someone get the phone."

Mrs. Easton picked up the receiver, asked who

it was, then looked toward George with her eyebrows raised.

"It's for Roxanne," she announced. George nodded and Mrs. Easton handed the phone to her daughter. Roxanne pulled the phone as far out into the hall as she could stretch the cord and placed it against her ear.

"Hello?" she asked.

"Hi, Roxanne," a warm voice replied across the wire.

"Oh, hi, Vince," Roxanne answered miserably.

"Listen, I've been out on a call with the rescue squad. I just need time to change, and then I'll be by to pick you up — "

"Wait, Vince," Roxanne interrupted. "I can't go."

"Why? Is something wrong?" His voice was filled with concern. "Are you sick?"

"Sick of my mother's boyfriend is more like it," she whispered. "He's grounded me because of the car accident!"

"Gee, it's kind of late for that, isn't it?"

"You're telling me!" Roxanne complained. "He just went berserk, and now I have to stay home for the entire weekend." Just saying it out loud sounded like a life sentence.

"That's awful," Vince said sympathetically. "You've been through so much already. I wish there were something I could do to help."

"No, there's nothing you can do. I'll just have to make the best of it." Roxanne sighed heavily, a hint of forlorn suffering creeping into her voice. "Well, you just have a good time with the gang at the sub shop, okay?"

"Naw, I couldn't go without you," Vince replied. "It wouldn't be the same. I'll stay home, too."

"Oh, now George has ruined your weekend, too," Roxanne said loudly, so they could overhear her in the living room. "It's just not fair!"

"Say, Roxanne, maybe we can make up for it next weekend."

"But that's the Fourth of July," Roxanne said, thinking ahead to the parade through Georgetown and the fireworks display.

"I know. Listen, every Fourth of July our whole family has their world-famous reunion," Vince announced proudly. "It's a great big picnic — lots of food, lots of people, and lots of fun."

"Oh?" Roxanne answered without really paying attention. She was already plotting her strategy for the coming week for getting back in with the crowd.

"Yeah, it's great!" Vince continued. "Uncle Paolo gets out his accordion and everybody sings and dances for hours. And my mom really prides herself on her homemade pasta — it's her big chance to show off. You're going to love all my brothers and sisters. And I'm sure they'll be crazy about you."

Roxanne's mind clicked back into the present tense. With a start she realized that her holiday was being planned out for her. And the plans sounded awful. A frantic picnic with a bunch of fat old men smoking smelly cigars and eating spaghetti, corny songs, and little kids running around screaming? No way! She searched quickly for a way out and found it.

"Oh, Vince, it does sound wonderful!" Roxanne gushed, hoping the phony sincerity in her voice wasn't too obvious. She lowered her voice so George wouldn't hear. "But, you see, I'm grounded next week, too."

"Oh, no!" Vince's disappointment showed plainly in his voice, and for just a fraction of a second Roxanne felt guilty about lying to him. But she soon got over it as she warmed to her new role of martyr.

"I know I have to take responsibility for what I did," she said, giving her voice a tremulous quiver. "It's just that it's such bad timing." Roxanne paused long enough to add a huge sob. "I would have *loved* to spend the weekend with your family."

Vince always turned to putty when she cried, and with a smile Roxanne realized it was much easier to fake over the phone than in person.

"Aw, Roxanne, please don't cry," Vince comforted. "There's always next year."

Roxanne almost laughed out loud. Next year? she thought to herself. Who was he kidding? As soon as she was back in the crowd, her relationship with Vince DiMase would be ancient history.

They said good-bye, and as soon as she hung up the receiver, Roxanne heaved a heartfelt sigh of relief. She was still furious with George for grounding her, but at least now she wouldn't have to endure that awful family picnic.

Roxanne strolled back into the living room and sat back down on the couch. Her mother and George were gone. They had left while she was on the phone. As usual, Jodi Easton had neglected to say good-bye to her daughter.

Torrey ignored her presence from his position in front of the TV. Another music video was blaring from the speakers, and Roxanne abruptly picked up the remote control and switched channels.

On cue her brother leaped up, ready to argue, but she silenced him with a warning look.

"Don't even think about it!" she snapped. "You've got nothing against me. Who would believe a juvenile delinquent like you?"

Torrey started to protest when she started in again. "Your derelict friends, however, would probably be very interested in hearing how amateurishly you took that corner." Roxanne paused dramatically to examine her nails. "They'd find that pretty funny . . . don't you think, Torrey? A big tough-guy like you not even able to handle a little bend in the road like that?"

Torrey's face went from an angry red to a fearful white to an ugly purple of frustrated rage. "That's — that's blackmail!" he sputtered.

Roxanne smiled sweetly and said, "You'd better believe it!"

Chapter
5

"What's wrong with this picture?" Brad Davidson muttered aloud. He was sitting by himself in one of the booths at the sub shop, surveying the usual Friday night bustle at his old high school hangout.

Kennedy High Cardinals football pennants still fluttered from the rafters above the old motorcycle that was hanging on the wall. As always, the old stuffed bear greeted newcomers as they walked through the door, and the air was filled with the tempting aroma of French fries and onion rings. Couples huddled in the back booths, while the unattached guys claimed a picnic table in the middle. Girls clustered about the table next to the jukebox, exchanging cracks with the boys. The music was blasting.

It was as if time had stood still. Without much effort Brad imagined himself, fresh from a student council meeting, notebook under his arm, eagerly stepping through the door to meet Brenda, who would have already been chatting away in this corner booth with some of the old crowd.

Brad squeezed his eyes shut and imagined Ted and Chris, Woody and Kim, Peter, Phoebe, and Sasha — all friends from his past, voting him in as class president and applauding his acceptance to Princeton.

"I know what's wrong," Brad said, sitting up with a start. "Me. I'm not the same anymore. I've changed."

He looked around the room at the tables full of kids, smiling and joking with each other, and realized he didn't recognize a soul. This only soured his mood further. Just then a quick burst of laughter from the door brought him out of his somber reverie and a big smile lit up his face.

Ted and Molly were struggling to squeeze through the front door beside Katie and Greg. All four of them were wedged in tight, giggling and laughing, until finally the logjam broke and they exploded into the sub shop. They spotted Brad and raced over to his booth.

"Boy, am I glad to see you guys!" Brad grinned warmly at his friends after they'd settled in around the worn table. "I was just starting to feel way too old and mature for this place."

"I guess we proved you wrong on that count," Greg chuckled.

Ted struck a pose like Abraham Lincoln and announced sagely, "You can take the kids out of Kennedy High, but you can't take Kennedy High out of the kids."

"What's that supposed to mean?" Katie demanded.

"It means you're never too old to steal your pals' French fries," Molly cracked, reaching over the table and scooping up a handful from Brad's basket.

"Same old Ramirez," Greg observed wryly. "The Bottomless Pit of Rose Hill."

Molly wrinkled her nose at him in reply and popped the fries into her mouth.

"So, what's new, guys?" Brad asked. "I feel like I've been in exile up in New Jersey." He tapped Ted on the shoulder and added, "How's it feel out at James Madison?"

Ted looked over at Molly with a grin and said emphatically, "I guarantee you, I'll be enjoying the fall in Virginia a lot more this year."

Molly smiled back at him, then explained, "I'm going to Mary Baldwin College in Staunton. It's really close to Harrisonburg, so Ted and I can see each other all the time."

"What about you two?" Brad asked, turning his attention to Greg and Katie.

Katie and Greg were sitting close together, like a pair of lovebirds. "We're trying not to think too much about the fall," Katie said, a little wistfully. "Just enjoying every minute we can until September. Then it's the U. of Florida for me."

Greg sighed dramatically, "And I will be carrying on at Kennedy High, trying to fill those size twelve shoes of yours as student body president. It's a dirty job — "

"But somebody's got to do it!" the others

50

finished for him. Ted stopped a waitress who was passing by, and they quickly ordered some more Cokes and fries.

"Well, I suppose you're all wondering why I called you here," Brad said with a grin, putting on his best student-body-president voice.

A chorus of boos rose up from the quartet around him, and Ted groaned, "No speeches, please!"

"Hey, I just thought you guys might be interested in a little Fourth of July backyard barbecue over at my house," Brad explained. "I've invited some fraternity brothers down from Princeton, and I thought it'd be a good opportunity for some of the old crowd to get together." He looked at them and shrugged, an amused glint in his eye. "But, hey, if no one's interested. . . ."

"Whoa, wait a minute!" Greg and Katie chorused.

"Yeah, who says we're not interested?" Ted demanded.

"Sounds great to me!" Molly enthused.

"It'd be nice to see some of the old guard again," Katie commented.

"I'm not sure who's around this summer," Ted cautioned, pensively stroking his chin. "Let's see . . . Phoebe and Michael are counselors at a music camp in Chapel Hill. Woody is a waiter at some hotel up in Vermont."

"Peter's on tour with that rock band, Jagged Edge," Katie piped up. "He's one of their roadies."

51

"Right. Sasha's still in town, though," Greg said, raising one finger. "I saw her down at her parent's bookstore last week."

"Chris is working as a congressional page in D.C., but I'll bet she'd come back to Rose Hill for the party," Katie added.

"And, of course, Brenda's in town," Molly said. "She's working in the psych department over at Georgetown."

Just hearing Brenda's name made Brad's throat tighten. They had broken up long before, but lately Brenda had been in his thoughts a lot. In high school they had been so different — Brad, decisive and determined, sure of what he wanted and not doubting for a second his ability to get it. Brenda was just the opposite — troubled, full of doubts, questioning everything, herself most of all. At the time it had been difficult for him to understand her attitude, but lately he seemed to be going through much of the same self-doubt.

"It'll be good to see Brenda again," he announced to the group. Then he added, half-jokingly, "Maybe with her new training in psychology, she can help me get over my angst."

"Your what?" Molly asked, a perplexed look on her face.

"Angst," Brad repeated. "One of those clever words you learn at college so you can come home and impress your friends who're still in high school."

"You impressed?" Greg asked Katie somberly. She shook her head and the two of them looked back at Brad.

"We're not impressed," they intoned, then burst

into laughter as Brad tossed his paper napkin at their grinning faces.

"So, what's it mean?" Molly demanded.

"It means — " Brad and Ted started to say together. Then Brad gestured to Ted and said, "After you, Dr. Freud."

Ted grinned and explained, "It's a psychological term for feeling vaguely anxious and gloomy, without an obvious reason."

"I guess it's just a simple case of the blues," Brad said lightly, ". . . or existential nausea."

"Oh, no!" Katie and Greg groaned, raising their hands in mock horror. "Not again!"

"All I can say," Molly interjected, staring down into her almost-empty basket of fries, "is if anyone decides to get nauseated around here, let me have their French fries."

"Who knows?" Greg kidded. "It might actually *be* the fries."

"You're kidding about all this, aren't you?" Ted asked, turning his attention back to Brad. "The only thing I can imagine you being anxious about is how you'll spend all the money you're going to earn when you're a doctor."

Brad shook his head. "I'm not even sure I want to *be* a doctor anymore."

"Aw, come on!" Ted let out an incredulous hoot of laughter and punched him on the arm. "You've had your medical career planned out since you were in third grade."

"Sounds like the Princetonian Sophomore Slump," Katie suggested sympathetically. "I hear it happens to everybody."

"Maybe." Brad shrugged and fell silent. How

could he explain it to his friends? Doubts just didn't happen to him. All his life he had been like a machine, methodically planning his goals and achieving them, one by one. Now, with six years left of school, and internship and residency looming before him in the future, Brad felt tired and uneasy.

"It's just. . . ." Brad groped for the right words to express his thoughts. "Well, I've never given myself any time to think — "

"Heap bad idea, Kemosabe," Greg broke in, wiggling his eyebrows warningly. "Never think. Might be catching."

The others laughed, but Brad just looked away uneasily.

The front door burst open and Jonathan sang out merrily, "That's okay, nobody get up! We can only stay a minute."

"And that's about a minute too long!" Ted shot back without skipping a beat.

"Hey! My man!" Jonathan approached the table, grinning from ear to ear, and gave Ted a high five. Then he turned and shook Brad's hand warmly.

"Say, Jonathan, who does your hair?" Molly asked, trying not to giggle. Little splotches of paint covered his whole body.

"I particularly like the rainbow effect," Kate drawled. "The purple and gold specks in your hair go well with the red and yellow globs on your face."

Jonathan looked momentarily befuddled, then glanced down at his paint-spattered shirt. "Oh, I get it," he said. "A bunch of wise guys, eh?"

"Looks like Jonathan isn't the only person who's sporting the latest summer colors," Molly remarked, pointing to Lily and Pamela, who had entered the sub shop with Jonathan and were standing near the takeout counter. They were both dressed in baggy coveralls and were splattered in paint from head to foot. A pretty, dark-haired girl wearing a men's chambray work shirt and Levi's was with them. For a second Brad didn't recognize her.

"Brenda. . . ." He barely whispered her name aloud. She looked more beautiful, more radiant than ever. Her personality seemed to light up the room. There was something new about her, in the confident way she stood, in the way she was speaking — her gestures definite and self-assured. Brad struggled to put his finger on what Brenda's special spark might be. Then it hit him. Happiness! She seemed happy with herself.

Brenda, Lily, and Pamela, picked up their orders and moved toward the door, stopping first at another table to talk with some of the newer kids. Brad leaped to his feet, nearly knocking the remains of his Coke over, and quickly crossed the room to greet her.

"Now, we need as many volunteers as we can get to help paint the wagons," Brenda was saying to the table of Kennedy High students as Brad came up beside her. He looked around the table and recognized Matt Jacobs, but the other faces were all unfamiliar to him. He stood there quietly, waiting for Brenda to notice him.

"We've got a couple of cars here," she went on, "and Jonathan's convertible will hold a lot of people, so —" Brenda stopped talking in mid-sentence when she saw Brad. A big, warm smile lit up her face as she set down her sandwiches and walked quickly around the end of the table.

Brad, grinning so hard his face hurt, met her and they hugged each other hard. "Wow! It's so good to see you," he said as Brenda wrapped her arms around his neck and squeezed him tight. "You look fantastic!"

"So do you!" Brenda said, stepping back and studying his face. "You're thinner, but still as handsome as ever."

"How's school?" he asked, not wanting to take his eyes off her for a minute.

"Good, good," she replied, bobbing her head up and down. "I'm going to Georgetown part-time and counseling part-time at Garfield House." She smiled happily and added, "It's working out really well."

"Good, good," Brad said. Then he realized he'd just repeated what she had said, and felt silly and giddy all at the same time. Frankly, he didn't care how he looked right now. He was just happy to see her.

"How about you?" she asked, her voice warm and relaxed. "Still head of the class?"

"Far from it," Brad said with a halfhearted chuckle. He shoved his hands into his pockets and cocked his head to look at her. Suddenly Brad was filled with an overwhelming certainty that Brenda could help him out of the hole he seemed to be digging for himself, if he could only talk to her.

"Listen, Brenda, I'd really like to spend some time with you," he began, his voice low and urgent. "How would you feel about going some place where we could talk?"

Brenda's eyes widened slightly with surprise. "I — I don't know," she replied. "I'd love to see you of course, but — "

"Yo, Austin!" Jonathan yelled from near the front door. "Let's go. The parade-mobile is leaving now."

"I'm on my way!" Brenda shouted back over her shoulder. Then she turned to Brad again, an apologetic smile on her face. "As you can see, I'm pretty wrapped up in this float we're building for Garfield House. We only stopped by to grab some suds and pick up a few recruits."

"I'm sorry. I should have noticed," Brad answered, staring down hard at the floor. "I didn't even think. Of course you'd have other plans." He suddenly felt embarrassed about nearly begging her to talk to him.

"Brad, it's okay, really," Brenda said quickly. "But maybe some time soon." On impulse she reached out and squeezed his arm. "Or how about joining us on the float crew? We can use any able-bodied person who can handle a paint brush."

Brad glanced over at the group from Kennedy High. They were all laughing and racing each other out the door. The last thing Brad wanted to do was spend the evening with a boisterous bunch of high school kids. He was already old, and if he went with them, he'd feel ancient by the end of the evening.

"Uh, no, thanks, Brenda," Brad replied. "But listen, I'm having a party this weekend. You know, sort of a reunion for the old gang, and —"

"I'll try to make it," Brenda answered hurriedly, waving toward the door and her waiting crew of helpers. "Maybe we can talk then, okay?" Without waiting for his answer, she turned and ran to join the others.

Brad stood alone in the middle of the sub shop, his hands jammed in his pockets. His feelings — about himself, about everything — were all tangled up in a confused jumble. Now, as he watched Brenda disappear around the corner, images of them together back in high school reverberated through his mind. They had shared some wonderful times.

You can't go home again, he reminded himself. Then he put his hands on his hips. Why not? The more he thought about it, the more Brad felt sure that the key to setting his life right again rested squarely with Brenda. If they could just get back together again, everything would work out.

Stacy watched as Brenda Austin charged out the front door of the sub shop, then stared forlornly at the empty soda cups and sub baskets littering the picnic table where she was sitting. Only moments ago, the table had been bustling with lively conversation and some spirited horsing around.

Josh, talking into a jar of Parmesan cheese, had improvised a crazy radio play. Matt Jacobs had gotten into a friendly argument with Daniel Tackett about rock and roll. He was convinced that if a song didn't sound great on a car radio, it wasn't fit to be called rock and roll. Daniel tried to make a case for rock having grown more subtle and sophisticated, but the fact that he was having to shout to make his voice heard above the jukebox diluted his argument.

Then Brenda had arrived and everyone had gone to help with the Garfield House float. Now Stacy was alone at the huge, empty table, which only seemed to emphasize the inescapable fact that Zack had stood her up.

Stacy took a sip of her Diet Coke and the straw made a loud slurping sound. She secretly wished the music would start up again so she wouldn't feel so conspicuous. She peeked at her Swatch watch again.

"Where is he?" she muttered under her breath. Stacy bit her lip in frustration. All week long she'd been looking forward to seeing him tonight. They had agreed to meet here — or had they? Okay, it hadn't been an official date, but the message had seemed clear enough at the time. If she'd be there, he'd be there.

Stacy felt her face redden as she thought of how excited she'd gotten at the prospect of seeing Zack tonight. She had tried on three different outfits before finally settling on the drop-waisted jean jumper and starched white shirt she was wearing now.

Obviously she'd been all wrong about Mr. Zachary McGraw. Stacy felt the hurt start to well up inside of her, and she clamped down on it like a vise. This is what happens, she thought angrily, when you let people know you care. She picked up one of the napkins and crumpled it into a tiny ball, then tossed it into a half-empty basket of fries.

That's it! Stacy decided abruptly. I'm leaving. She slammed her empty cup down on the table and stood up, crashing right into the guy Brenda Austin had been talking to just before she left.

"I'm really sorry," the handsome boy apologized. "I wasn't paying attention."

"No, no, it was my fault," Stacy said quickly, feeling like a complete idiot. "I bumped into you. Sometimes I'm such a klutz!"

Before they could offer any more apologies, Katie Crawford joined them. "Ah, Brad, I see you've met my star student." They both turned to stare at Katie, who laughed and introduced them. "Brad Davidson, meet Stacy Morrison, Rose Hill's brightest hope for the Junior Olympics."

"Oh?" Brad looked down at Stacy, obviously impressed. "In what?"

"Discus throwing," Stacy cracked with a straight face.

Brad paused momentarily, noticing her diminutive frame, then grinned at the joke. "Right!"

"She's our best new gymnast," Katie explained. "Listen, Stace, I noticed you were sitting alone. Why don't you come join us?" Katie gestured toward the corner booth where Greg and Ted were still sitting. "Unless, of course, you're waiting for someone."

"No, I wasn't waiting for anyone," Stacy said quickly. "No one at all. I'd love to join you."

As she turned to follow them to the corner, Stacy looked back at the door once more to see if

Zack had come in, but there was no sign of him.

Stop it! she warned herself angrily. You're being a fool! Then and there Stacy decided to banish all thoughts of Zachary McGraw from her mind forever. She made a secret vow with herself never to drop her defenses with a guy again. Now, more than ever, she knew her wise-guy attitude was the best way to approach life. If they can't get near you, she thought grimly, they can't hurt you.

Chapter
6

The following Monday morning, Frankie paused to blow a strand of blonde hair out of her eyes before renewing her efforts to polish the sleek brass railing in front of her. It promised to be a long day. The swank decor of the Foxy Lady boutique included endless railings, all glistening brass, all needing constant attention. She wiped the perspiration on her forehead away with the back of her hand and sat up straight, stretching her already-aching back. Just then, Frankie caught a glimpse of herself in one of the full-length mirrors lining the wall and nearly laughed out loud.

"Glamorous job, my foot!" she snorted at her reflection. She'd only been at the Foxy Lady a week, but already she'd gone from salesgirl to resident cleaning lady.

Keeping the trendy store looking its best was a full-time job, too. The ground floor showrooms were covered in plush white carpeting, with sleek matching couches that seemed to attract dirt like a magnet. The slender mannequins, sporting the store's latest sportswear creations, were black and gleamed like polished porcelain in the windows. Little splashes of crimson accented the glossy white walls of the shop, and a single red rose in a vase by the cashier's counter added just the right touch of chic elegance.

"You know, it's really you!" The all-too-familiar voice carried above the low murmur of voices in the store. Frankie glanced over toward the sound to catch Roxanne, stunningly dressed in a loose white silk chemise draped over a matching skirt and pumps, helping a rather plump older woman pick out a bathing suit.

The woman headed toward the dressing room. Roxanne waited until the lady was out of sight, then turned toward the other salegirls clustered around the register. Pointing in the customer's direction, she rolled her eyes and silently mooed like a cow. The salesgirls all giggled, then slapped at each other, trying to stifle their laughter.

The salesgirls all looked like models, and although Roxanne was a good deal younger than the others, Frankie noticed that she seemed to fit in quite nicely. Too nicely, in fact. Although they had both been hired as salesgirls, within a few days Roxanne had cajoled and badgered Frankie into taking over all of her more menial responsibilities, leaving Roxanne more time to work the sales floor.

Frankie resented being pushed around like that, but on the other hand, it was kind of a relief not having to work much with the customers. She knew she wasn't very good at it.

Frankie took another look at herself in the mirror. She was holding a dusty, dirty rag in her hand and somehow had managed to get a smudge of dust across her nose. "You most definitely do not fit in down here," she told her reflection.

Frankie made a quick check around the store, then moved toward the back stairs that led to the workroom above the shop. Opening the door at the top of the stairs, she felt the temperature shift abruptly from the cool of the air-conditioned store to the humid, muggy atmosphere of the workroom. An old window fan clanked loudly at the far end of the narrow attic room, and individual fans revolved back and forth at the various work stations. Even so, they didn't seem to be having much effect on the temperature.

Frankie paused and listened to the rhythmic clatter of the five sewing machines. Every now and then the sound of scissors snipping the thread and the slap of metal hitting metal as they were laid back down, punctuated the steady drone of the machines.

The seamstresses were mostly middle-aged women, except for a young girl named Kim, who'd emigrated recently from Korea. Each woman had a bandanna around her head to keep the perspiration from stinging her eyes. Mrs. Mendez, the shop foreman, patrolled the center aisle, making sure that each station was supplied with new bobbins of thread and pieces of material to be sewn together.

Frankie shook her head. No matter how you

looked at it, the Foxy Lady was a sweatshop right out of the nineteenth century. The working conditions were terrible for these women, but they didn't have much of a choice. Most could barely speak English and really couldn't have gotten another job. When Frankie asked if they felt they were being unfairly used, the women all insisted they were grateful to have a job at all.

In spite of the heat and noise, Frankie did feel more at home upstairs, sweeping up the scraps of material and delivering new bolts to the cutters who worked at the long tables at the back of the room. There was a lack of pretension up here that was refreshing after being downstairs and watching the salesgirls cater to the wealthy, sometimes snobby customers.

All in all, however, Frankie had to admit her job wasn't too bad. Using her first paycheck, she had already made a down payment on her new computer. Frankie smiled as she thought of the XB70 that would be hers by the end of summer.

"Frankie!"

The slender teen looked up to see the shop foreman gesturing to her. She made her way down the aisle, stopping to pick up some discarded bits of material off the floor and stuff them in the scrap bin.

"*Si, Señora Mendez, que quiere usted?* What do you want?" Frankie asked the older woman. She tried to practice her Spanish every chance she could with Mrs. Mendez, who always got a big kick out of Frankie's terrible accent. The woman grinned at Frankie and pointed toward a rack of new clothes. They were all finished and ready to be taken downstairs and put on display. Frankie nodded, looped her fingers beneath the hangers, and made her way toward the stairs.

The gentlest tinkling of a bell signaled that a customer had entered the store. At the landing, Frankie paused to take a breather and caught a glimpse of the newcomer — Vince DiMase. He was standing near the register, holding a large spray of wildflowers and talking to Roxanne.

"Oh, Vince, you shouldn't have. Really," she heard Roxanne say.

"I was doing some rock climbing around the base of the Pinnacle," Vince mumbled, looking around as if he didn't quite believe he was in this strange, exotic place. "You know, south of Front Royal, along the Appalachian Trail?"

Roxanne looked at him blankly, and Vince shifted his weight uneasily. He was still in his climbing gear, heavy boots with thick cotton socks, weathered canvas shorts, and a T-shirt.

"These grow all over the place down there," he said, a crooked grin on his face. "I thought you'd like them."

"They're beautiful," Roxanne said softly, almost in a whisper.

Frankie watched their exchange and felt a tug at her heart. Vince seemed so sweet. There was no phony pretense to him at all. He was what he was, unabashedly and unashamedly. Could he really have gotten through to Roxanne? She seemed to be really moved by his thoughtful gesture. Maybe she really had changed.

"Hi, Vince," Frankie called from the foot of the stairs. "Welcome to the Foxy Lady." She was still holding the pile of clothes in her arms and raised it in greeting.

"Hi, Frankie," Vince said, flashing a big smile at her.

Frankie could tell by the look on his face that he was genuinely relieved to see her.

Frankie hung the newly made clothes on the rack, making sure to arrange them according to size and with the hangers all facing the same direction, then wheeled the rack over to the cash register.

"Introduce us to your boyfriend," said Bev Delaney, the store manager, slinking up to join Roxanne. She was dressed in a peach-colored silk suit, with matching shoes and nail polish. Frankie figured Bev's apartment must look like a beauty salon, filled with hair spray, curling irons, shoe racks, and lipsticks of every shade imaginable.

"Vince DiMase, this is Bev Delaney," Roxanne said. "Bev is my supervisor."

"And I am her co-worker," Nicole Bird said, stepping in to join the group.

Vince shook Bev's hand. "Pleased to meet you, ma'am." Then he nodded politely to Nicole.

Bev and Nicole raised their eyebrows at each other and then turned back to stare unashamedly at Vince. They definitely found him attractive, and their smiles reflected it.

Vince shoved his hands in the pockets of his shorts and smiled nervously at each of the women. Frankie thought he looked a little like a lamb in a cage full of lionesses.

Finally he shrugged and announced "Well, I guess I'd better be going." He spun around and walked directly into the rack of clothes Frankie had placed by the cash register.

Roxanne yelled "Look out!" but it was too late. The rack lay on the floor with a jumble of tangled hangers and clothes scattered around it.

"I'll fix it!" Frankie yelled, springing to Vince's rescue.

"I'm really sorry," Vince said, setting the rack upright. "Sometimes I can be so clumsy!"

"It's okay," Frankie said, taking the mass of hangers from him. "If you hadn't knocked it over, I probably would have."

Vince flashed her a grateful, mortified smile and backed toward the door. "I guess I do better in wide open spaces." He was about to crash into another rack when a woman's squeal stopped him cold.

"I didn't know there was a man in here!" the overweight woman in a way-too-small bathing suit shrieked.

Instantly Vince shielded his eyes and mumbled, "There isn't. I was just leaving."

"One of you girls should have warned me," the woman huffed as she pulled frantically at the wrong dressing room door.

Bev, stifling a laugh, scurried over to assist her. She made cooing sounds as the woman muttered, "I've never been so embarrassed in my life."

Vince apologized to everyone. "Please forgive my intrusion. Next time, I'll meet Roxanne outside." He flashed a shy smile at the ladies and waved good-bye.

Roxanne, still clutching the bouquet, walked with him to the door.

"Listen," Vince said. "I'll call you later, okay?"

"Sure," Roxanne said with a quick nod. Then Vince brushed her cheek with a kiss and was gone.

"Well, well, well," Nicole commented with a dry laugh, "it appears that chivalry is not dead, after all."

"Where in the world did you dig up a guy like that?" Bev remarked. "I thought his type went out with the dinosaurs!"

The sound of the girls' teasing made Roxanne spin around, her cheeks suddenly red. She seemed embarrassed, Frankie thought, but she recovered quickly. She held the bouquet out at arm's length and grimaced.

"Can you believe that hick," she groaned, "bringing me this bunch of weeds? I'll probably get hay fever or something."

"Oh, I don't know. I think he's kind of cute," Nicole said, swinging her dark hair.

"Sure he's cute," Roxanne shot back, "if you're into Cro-Magnon men." The other girls laughed with her, and Rox relaxed. Warming to her audience, she added, "Believe me, his looks are the only reason we're together."

"I can tell you're really suffering," Bev remarked, a wry grin on her face.

"More than you know!" Roxanne said emphatically. "Get this — he wanted me to go to his family reunion picnic this weekend."

"So?" Nicole shrugged. "What's so bad about that? You should go."

"What?" Roxanne almost shrieked. "And listen to his uncle sing dopey old songs while his mother tries to get everyone to stuff themselves?

Both Nicole and Bev groaned loudly, and Roxanne added, "And he thought I'd love it. Can you believe it?"

"Not exactly *my* idea of a fun date," a girl named Evelyn, who'd just come in from the back room, chipped in.

"Especially on the Fourth of July," Roxanne said, tossing the bouquet in the wastebasket behind the counter. Then she dropped her voice and giggled. "I got out of it by pretending I'd been grounded, and naive guy that he is, he completely fell for it!"

The other girls shrieked with laughter. Nicole, however, wasn't laughing. "I don't know," she said, trying to override their giggles. "I thought he seemed really nice."

"Exactly!" Roxanne pounced on her comment like a tiger. "He's *too* nice. I mean, what fun is nice? It's about as interesting as oatmeal. Give me exciting, or sexy, or *dangerous!*"

The other girls squealed delightedly, egging her on. Their laughter grated on Frankie's nerves, and she could feel her insides churning.

"Take if from me, girls," Roxanne declared, "Vince DiMase is just a little detour along the line for me, until the real thing comes along!"

Frankie turned and walked stiffly back up the stairs. How could anyone be so cruel? As the laughter faded in her ears, she thought, *Roxanne has changed, all right. She's now beyond hope.*

Chapter
7

"Let's try the entire sequence again," Katie called across the deserted gymnasium to Stacy, who was bent over by the edge of the blue tumbling mat, trying to catch her breath. "The aerial cartwheel was great, but you untucked a little too soon in the back flip."

Stacy shook her head, frustrated with her performance. She and Katie had been hard at work for the past two hours, repeating the same series of moves over and over again. They had the second floor gym at the Fitness Center entirely to themselves this Saturday afternoon, and Katie had put Stacy through her paces relentlessly.

"All right, Coach," Stacy said, lifting herself back to an upright position. "You're the boss." She stepped lightly onto the gym floor and walked resolutely back to her position at the corner of the large blue mat.

Stacy closed her eyes and took a deep breath to

center herself. She took a moment to imagine the perfect execution of the moves she intended to do — an aerial cartwheel, two steps into a round-off, back handspring, and finally the double back flip. Then she opened her eyes, spotted herself and, raising up on her toes, pounded across the blue mat.

From the first leap, Stacy knew she had nailed the sequence. Exploding out of the handspring into the flip, she expertly tucked herself into a little ball. This time she forced herself to wait a fraction of a second longer to unfold. It worked. She landed with both feet planted firmly on the ground.

"Bravo!" Katie said, clapping her hands enthusiastically and leaping up off the bleachers to come join her protégée. "If you can get yourself to concentrate like that every time, there's no one in this league who can touch you!"

Stacy's cheeks flushed with pleasure at the high praise. Katie's approval meant a lot to her because she knew more than most people how high Katie's standards were.

"How do you feel?" Katie asked, tossing a dry towel into Stacy's arms.

"Okay," Stacy answered with a shy shrug.

"Okay? Just okay?" Katie let a hoot of laughter and shook her finger at Stacy in mock anger. "You little liar! You know you feel great!"

Stacy giggled and then nodded emphatically. She felt like flying! She had such an incredible thrill of accomplishment when she'd pushed herself to the limit — and broken through. Finding the discipline within herself to keep at it had always been a problem for Stacy, but with Katie goading her on, she had found the drive.

"Boy, Katie," Stacy said, flopping cross-legged on the mat and vigorously toweling her hair, "I don't know what I'm going to do when you go to Florida this fall."

"You'll do just fine," Katie said, hitching up her sweatpants and joining her friend on the mat. "The key is to maintain your discipline. Don't ease up on yourself."

"Discipline is what I'm worried about," Stacy said, frowning slightly.

"Well, if I see that you've slacked off when I come back to Rose Hill at Christmas," Katie joked, "I'll let you have it, big time!"

Stacy smiled and watched as Katie spread her legs into a split, wincing just a little bit, and bent forward to touch her chest to one knee. Then Katie rotated to face center, carefully easing toward the mat, trying to regain the flexibility she had lost since she broke her leg in a skiing accident six months before. Up until then, Katie had been a champion gymnast.

All those dreams had ended in a few painful seconds on the slopes. Katie had endured some really rough times since then, trying to come out of her depression and disappointment. Finally she had turned her formidable energies to coaching Stacy, trying to turn the younger girl from a talented but haphazard athlete into a focused, tough competitor. The relationship had been good for both of them.

"Katie, can I ask you something?" Stacy said suddenly. "Personal, I mean."

Katie looked up sharply, a little surprised. Then she shrugged and nodded.

"How did you manage to stay so focused?" Stacy asked slowly, "It must be so hard, with school and Greg. . . ."

Katie thought for a second, kneading her calf with her knuckles, then said simply, "A lot of times it *is* hard, juggling training, homework, and your love life." She smiled and said, "You have to learn to balance your priorities. Each one demands more attention at different times." She grimaced a little and added, "And not always at the best time for other people, either."

"How does Greg feel about that?"

"Well, luckily for me, Greg is a disciplined athlete himself," Katie replied. "He understands better than most people about sticking to a training regimen."

"You guys sure are lucky to have each other," Stacy said, unable to keep the wistfulness out of her voice. "Was it hard getting together?"

"Getting together was easy," Katie said, her mouth widening into a grin. "Staying together was the hard part."

Stacy tilted her head in confusion. "I don't get it."

"How can I explain this?" Katie's eyes twinkled with amusement. "Greg and I — well, we both have . . . strong personalities." She laughed and added, "We've been known to bump heads in the past."

"But you guys always worked it out, right?" Stacy persisted. "I mean, you seem so perfect together now."

"Yeah, we're a good team." Katie nodded, then bent forward quickly to hide the tears suddenly misting her eyes. After struggling so hard, she and Greg had finally found each other again, just in time for her to head for Florida. Sometimes life just wasn't fair.

Katie leaped abruptly to her feet. "Speaking of Mr. Greg Montgomery, I have a date to meet him right about now." She turned to Stacy and said, "You can continue without me, can't you?"

Stacy nodded but dropped her gaze, trying to hide the disappointment in her eyes.

"Okay, listen up!" Katie put her hands on her hips and sternly instructed, "I advise you to work on your adagio on the balance beam. Don't push yourself, keep it nice and easy. And then hit the showers!"

Stacy hopped up beside her and snapped to attention. "Is that an order, Coach?"

Katie laughed and nodded. "That's an order!" She grabbed her own towel from the bench and trotted off toward the women's locker room.

Stacy watched her friend leave and, suddenly filled with great determination, moved toward the far wall and the balance beam. She slipped on her soft, leather jazz shoes and stepped into the resin box. Then she nimbly leaped onto the wooden beam in a straddle mount, smoothly turning into a split with her left arm gracefully arched above her head.

Let's see, Stacy thought to herself, which ballet will it be today? She floated through her adagio movements — a series of slow, precise moves — concentrating on fluidity and elegance.

Knowing that no one was watching her made it easy for Stacy to put her heart into her routine. There was no need to hide behind the shell of indifference she always put up against the world.

Of course! Swan Lake, she thought. Imagining herself in the role of Odette, the beautiful swan from the familiar ballet, she gracefully moved from a backward somersault into an arabesque on one knee, her other leg extended high behind her.

Humming to herself, she fluttered her arms as if they were floating through water. When she reached the end of the beam, Stacy paused for a moment, reaching toward the ceiling, then slowly arched into a back bend and walkover.

She was in a dream world, a world, of her own creation. Her eyes shining, Stacy spun and bourréed in delicate little steps back down the beam.

Something moved out of the corner of her eye, breaking her concentration. A guy was standing in the doorway of the gym — watching her make a fool of herself! Quickly Stacy bounded off the beam and did a couple of clownish cartwheels across the floor, toward the intruder.

When she finally came to a bouncing stop, Stacy found herself staring directly into a pair of soulful blue eyes. They belonged to Zachary McGraw.

"I didn't mean to interrupt your workout." Zack ran his hand through his blond hair and mumbled, "Guess I got a little lost."

He was wearing maroon running shorts and a crisp white tank top. The pale green strap of his workout bag stood out in deep contrast to his tanned, muscular shoulder.

Stacy could hardly catch her breath. She didn't know whether to be angry or glad. Funny things were happening to her all at once. Her knees felt awfully wobbly, and try as she might, she couldn't keep herself from gazing dumbly into his warm blue eyes.

"You see, I was looking for the weight room," Zack explained, his words spilling out in an awkward rush. "I just joined this center. I used to go to a gym near Stevenson, but I figured since I'm at Kennedy now, I should start coming here and work out with the rest of the guys — "

"The weight room is on the next floor," Stacy said, cutting him off.

Zack's eyes widened in surprise at her rudeness. Then he said, "Thanks." There was an awkward pause as they looked at each other. "Well, um, sorry I disturbed you," Zack finally muttered. "I'm off."

As he backed away toward the exit, already looking a little stung, Stacy couldn't resist tossing out another barb.

"You know, I'm really surprised a big star jock like you would lower yourself to be seen working out with the Kennedy crowd." He looked up at her, stunned, and she pressed on. "I mean, you can't even bring yourself to hang out at the sub shop. What's the matter, isn't that good enough for Mr. All-City Football Star?"

"The sub shop?" Zack repeated, his hand frozen on the door. Then the realization crept across his face. "Were you there on Friday?"

77

Stacy's defiant look answered his question.

"Gee, Stacy, I . . . I'm really sorry," Zack stammered. "I thought — "

"It doesn't matter," Stacy said indifferently. "No one missed you — least of all me. In fact, I stayed real late and had a *wonderful* time."

Zack didn't answer, but looked at her curiously. "You waited for *me?*" he asked slowly.

Stacy snorted derisively. "Don't flatter yourself. I was having a good time with the gang, so I hung around."

"But I heard everybody left early to go help out at Garfield House," Zack said doubtfully. "Why didn't you go with them?"

"Well, I . . . I don't know!" Stacy couldn't think of anything to say. Her cheeks started to burn. Furious at herself for being such a wimp, she spun on her heels and marched back to the bench, where she had tossed her towel. Her heart pounded in her chest as she listened, hoping to hear Zack's footsteps fade away as he left the gym. But the only sound that came was that of the door to the gym swinging shut with a gentle "swoosh."

Zack stepped lightly across the floor toward her. The squeak of his court shoes alerted Stacy to his presence and her back stiffened as he came nearer. Stacy didn't turn around.

"You know, uh, I caught some of your routine on the beam," Zack began, his voice echoing unusually loudly around the drafty gymnasium. "You looked just like a ballerina up there."

Stacy whirled around, her eyes flashing, searching his face for the mockery she was certain she'd find there. To her surprise his eyes glistened with unabashed admiration.

Zack cleared his throat softly. "I can count on one hand the times I've seen an athlete — *any* athlete — put so much of him- or herself into a workout. Your concentration is. . . ." He groped for the right words, finally saying, "Awesome!"

Stacy sat slowly down on the bench. She didn't know how to respond to him and it was driving her crazy. Why was it that every time she was up close to Zack, she lost her ability to stay cool, to pull back? He completely unnerved her. It was maddening.

"Stacy?" Zack sat down on the bench beside her, a little distance away. "Why did you tell me on the beach that gymnastics was no big deal to you?"

His voice was warm and open, without a trace of criticism in it. Stacy felt more lost than ever. She studied her hands for a what seemed like an eternity, then answered him with a shrug.

"The girl I saw just now," he said softly, "dancing on that balance beam . . . she seemed to love what she was doing more than anything else in the world."

They sat still for a moment, neither of them moving a muscle. Finally Stacy confessed, "I guess sometimes I pretend not to care about things." Her voice rang tinny and very small in her ears, as though it were coming from far, far away. "Especially things that are important to me."

Zack nodded and smiled ruefully. "I think I understand that one. It's sort of like me and school."

Stacy tilted her head to look up at him curiously. "What do you mean?"

"You see, all my dad cares about is how well I do in football, or basketball, or whatever's in season," Zack said. "So he tells me not to worry about studying. I know I should do better in school, and I want to. I think I can, but. . . ." This time he shrugged. "Studying isn't easy for me, so I pretend it doesn't matter."

Now he was staring at his hands. Stacy noticed his powerful wrists, the long fingers, full of strength, yet somehow gentle. Then she looked back up and their eyes met. This time she didn't look away. Neither did Zack.

"I'm sorry I didn't show up at the sub shop," Zack said quietly, his eyes wide and vulnerable. "I didn't think you were serious about meeting me."

Stacy couldn't stand the pressure of his gaze anymore. She averted her eyes and said blithely, "I wasn't."

"Oh." He was silent for a moment. "Because I would have gone," Zack said finally, "if I'd known you were going to be there."

"Really?" Stacy's voice was barely a whisper in her throat. She willed herself to look up at him, and Zack nodded gently.

Stacy swallowed hard, then said, "Zack, I have a confession to make."

"What's that?" he asked.

"I *was* waiting for you at the sub shop," she blurted out quickly.

Zack's handsome face widened into a smile. "You were?" he said hopefully.

"Of course I was," Stacy retorted. "Why do you think I didn't go with everyone over to Garfield House?"

Zack didn't answer. He simply grinned at her, a silly chuckle bubbling up out of his throat.

"In fact," Stacy said, crossing her arms and squinting at him, "I wasted an entire evening, waiting for you — you big lug!"

At that, Zack burst out laughing. His laughter was infectious, and soon Stacy was giggling, too.

"Listen, I think I owe you one," Zack said finally. "If I promise to show up, will you meet me on the Fourth for the big parade?"

"I'll go you one better," Stacy replied, feeling reckless and giddy at the same time. "If you show up for the parade, I'll show up for the fireworks afterward!"

"It's a deal!" Zack instinctively moved closer to Stacy on the bench and smiled directly into her bright eyes.

Stacy could feel the warmth of his shoulder against her arm and she held her breath waiting for him to kiss her.

Zack leaned ever so slightly closer to her, and an electric thrill shot up her leg as his knee touched hers.

Stacy leaned gently toward him and waited. Everything was still, the only sound in the gym was their breathing and Stacy's heart pounding in her ears. The two of them were frozen like statues, waiting.

Stacy's face suddenly flushed a deep crimson as she realized that they were both waiting for the other to make the first move.

The thought struck Zack at the same moment, and he abruptly stood up, nearly falling across Stacy in the process. She let out a loud embarrassed giggle that seemed to echo endlessly around the gymnasium.

Zack, whose own face had started to flush red, chuckled at what had just happened. Then his chuckle turned into a hearty laugh, and he held out his hand, "Let's shake on it."

Stacy grasped his hand in hers, and Zack pulled her lightly to her feet. Their awkward moment had passed and still holding onto Zack's hand, Stacy walked him to the gym door.

"See you on the Fourth!" Stacy called as he stepped through the big wooden doors.

Zack turned around and saluted. "It's a date!"

The door swung shut with a whoosh, and Stacy squeezed her eyes shut and counted to sixty. After a full minute had passed, she opened her sparkling eyes wide and shouted, "A date!"

Then she let out a loud whoop and ran with all her might toward the blue tumbling mat. She dove into a round-off and then did three back handsprings in a row. At the very end of the long mat she bounced in the air and, slapping her thighs, shouted, "I've got a date!"

Chapter
8

"I love a parade!" Roxanne sang loudly. She put the last touches on the piece she was working on and laid the finished red-white-and-blue sash on the pile with the others. With each passing minute, her spirits seemed to soar higher and higher. Watching her, Frankie wondered why Rox was in such a good mood.

"What'd you say?" Frankie shouted at her over the rat-a-tat of her own machine. The two of them had been in the attic workshop of the Foxy Lady since seven o'clock that morning.

Roxanne lifted her foot off the pedal of her machine and yelled back, "I said, I can't wait for the parade today!"

Frankie looked up at her in surprise. "You're not planning to go, are you?"

"Well, of course I'm going," Roxanne replied. "Why wouldn't I?" Roxanne picked up a piece of red material and lined it up with a blue one.

"I don't get it," Frankie said, shaking her head. "I thought you told Vince you were grounded this weekend."

"I did, but that was just to get out of that dreary picnic," Roxanne explained. "Believe me, I have no intention of staying home today!"

"But what if he sees you at the parade?"

"He won't see me," Roxanne said confidently. "He's spending the entire day with the whole DiMase clan, listening to *old* people tell endless stories about the *old* country, playing *old* songs on *old* accordions." Every time she said "old," Roxanne turned the sash she was sewing. "Besides, what he doesn't know won't hurt him." She held up another finished sash. "*Voilà!*"

"But what if he finds out you lied to him?" Frankie asked.

"I can handle it," Roxanne said blithely, dismissing the thought with an airy wave of her arm. "I always do."

Frankie shook her head in disapproval. She focused her attention back on the sash she was sewing, letting Roxanne's words sink in. When she had finished the sash, she folded it neatly and put it on the pile, then reached for three more swatches of material.

Frankie hadn't planned on helping Roxanne with the sashes at all. She had been skeptical about the idea from the beginning, sure that this was yet another one of Roxanne's attempts to get back into the crowd's good graces. But when Brenda Austin had discovered that Frankie worked at the Foxy Lady too, the older girl had assumed that Frankie would help Roxanne out.

And Frankie had to admit that once she knew the crowd needed the sashes, she felt personally responsible for making sure Roxanne came through with the goods.

"That brings our grand total to nineteen," Roxanne announced, counting the pile of sashes she had stacked on the table beside her. "With the one you're sewing now, we'll have an even twenty."

"I think we should make a few more," Frankie said as she picked up the scissors and snipped the thread on her sash. "Just in case more members of the gang show up."

Roxanne sighed impatiently and checked her brand-new Swatch. It was red, white, and blue. In fact, now that Frankie thought about it, she saw that Roxanne had concentrated extra hard on coming up with a way to stand out during the parade. Even though Josh had provided the gang with colorful paper overalls, Roxanne had cannily bought herself a red-and-white striped pair that would fit right in if they asked her to march. As an added flourish, she'd worn a pair of bright red tennis shoes, with blue-and-white laces. Her white sailor-collared blouse, with big blue bow, would look adorable as they marched along the parade route.

"Look, if we don't hurry, we'll miss the parade completely," Roxanne declared. Abruptly she switched off her machine and began piling the sashes into a black-and-red Foxy Lady shopping bag. Then she hurried toward the stairs.

Frankie hurriedly ran up a final seam on the last of the sashes, flipped off her sewing machine, and moved to follow Roxanne. Roxanne's next words froze her in her tracks.

"Oh, Frankie, look at the mess!" Roxanne pointed at the scraps of material littering the floor. "This shop is a disaster! What if George comes by and sees it?"

"He'd hit the roof," Frankie answered glumly, remembering how angry George had been last Tuesday when he'd stopped by the boutique and discovered a few stray hangers on the floor by one of the dressing rooms.

"He'd fire us both," Roxanne said in ominous tones.

Frankie didn't doubt it for a minute. She quickly set her purse down and moved to get a broom. "You're right. We'd better clean it up."

"Oh, would you?" Roxanne said in her grateful kitten voice. "That would be terrific! Then I can deliver the sashes on time."

"Now, hold it, just a minute!" Frankie snapped, immediately tossing the broom back into the corner. "I said *we'd* better clean up. We *both* made this mess and we *both* should clean it up!"

Roxanne didn't budge an inch. Instead she glanced down at her watch impatiently. "Look, Frankie, be reasonable." Her voice was brusque and businesslike. "It's getting late. One of us really should get down to Garfield House with the sashes so they can be handed out to the marchers. And since I have the car, I think it's only logical that I be the one to go."

Frankie could feel hot beads of perspiration ripple across her forehead. "I cannot believe this is happening to me — again!" she muttered through clenched teeth. Frankie wanted to run out into the street and scream with fury. The trouble was, she knew George really would fire them if he came by. And if she lost her job, she'd lose her deposit on the computer. She didn't have any choice but to give in.

"Did it ever occur to you, Roxanne," Frankie said bitterly, slumping against the wall, "that maybe I might want to go to the parade, too?"

"Well, if that's all you're worried about," Roxanne cooed, slipping her arm around Frankie's shoulder, "then there's absolutely no problem. Look, I'll just dash over to Garfield House, drop off the sashes — saving two for us, of course — and then dash right back here and get you." She gave Frankie an affectionate, encouraging squeeze. "It'll be a little tight, but we won't miss the parade. Okay?"

With all her heart, Frankie wanted to believe Roxanne was being sincere. "Okay," she mumbled, trying to ignore the knot of doubt forming in the pit of her stomach.

"I knew you'd understand," Roxanne said, heading quickly for the stairs. As she disappeared down the steps, she wiggled her fingers above her head without looking back. "Be back in a flash!"

Frankie slumped down against the wall again, as Roxanne went down the stairs, through the store, and out the front door. The tinkle of the bell as the front door closed roused her out of her daze. Frankie realized she had only a short time to clean up. Grabbing the broom, she attacked the huge pile of scraps with a vengeance.

* * *

A thick crowd was already milling around the brick entrance to Garfield House when Roxanne pulled her mother's rental car into the parking lot. As she stepped out onto the pavement, she glimpsed Jonathan and Lily off to the side, megaphones in hand, busily teaching the bleary-eyed marchers their routines. Both of them were wearing wild Hawaiian shirts under their paper coveralls.

"Listen up, everybody!" Lily yelled, "March right means when you lead *only* with your right foot, pulling the other behind you."

Jonathan demonstrated by hobbling around in a circle, dragging his left foot after him.

"You look like the Hunchback of Notre Dame," Matt Jacobs called out from his borrowed truck. On the door was hung a big, brightly colored sign that said, "Garfield House." Behind the truck was a wagon filled with the strangest collection of rock musicians ever assembled.

They were all outfitted in authentic Colonial dress, complete with powdered wigs, waistcoats, and breeches. Each person stood behind electric guitars, drums, and synthesizers, and the logo on the bass drum read, "The Founding Fathers." A big banner circling the wagon proclaimed the title of their entry: "We Built This Country On Rock 'n' Roll!"

Roxanne giggled as she read the namecards attached to each of the musicians. The lead guitarist, a tall redhead, wore a banner beneath his Gibson Flying Vee guitar, saying, "Thomas Jefferson Starship." Next to him stood "Andrew Thriller Jackson" with a bass guitar. "John

Adams Ant" peered out from behind a bank of Roland synthesizers.

It was all really impressive. Brian had rigged a powerful sound system so the "Presidents" could lip-synch their way along the parade route. The speakers were already pounding out some hot tunes, and people were dancing in the street as they completed the final preparations on the float's decor. Roxanne recognized the artwork as Pamela Green's, but it looked like everyone had really pitched in, adding their own personal touches.

The sashes will be the pièce de résistance, she thought proudly, tying it all together!

"Hey, everybody!" Roxanne called out to the marchers, trying to get their attention. "I've brought the sashes!"

"Marchers, 'Parade Rest!'" Jonathan bellowed out at the top of his lungs. Fifteen marchers dropped immediately to the ground. Everyone burst out laughing.

Lily and Jonathan, both a little stunned that Roxanne had made good on her promise, ran over to greet her.

"Hey, these are fantastic!" Lily sang out, slipping one of the colorful bands of material over her head. "You did a great job, Rox."

"Thanks," Roxanne replied, remembering to look humble. "Oh, I made a few extras, too. Just in case any more of your gang show up." She made sure to say "your" this time.

Jonathan cocked his head at her in pleased surprise. "That was really thoughtful of you," he said, beaming his approval. "Look, why don't you put one of these on and march up at the front with us?"

"Me? Really?" Roxanne asked, her green eyes shining with delight. Things were working out better than she'd ever dreamed.

"Sure!" Jonathan enthused. "The steps aren't hard. Just stumble along with everyone else." He gestured for her to follow him back to the waiting marchers. "Oh, make sure Josh gives you a kazoo!"

At the mention of Josh's name, Roxanne suddenly remembered Frankie back at the Foxy Lady, waiting for Roxanne to come pick her up. Hurriedly she checked her watch. The parade would begin in half an hour. There wasn't enough time to get Frankie and make it back before the start of the parade.

No sense in both of us missing the parade, Roxanne reasoned to herself. Frankie'll just have to understand. She'd explain everything to Josh — sort of — when she went to pick up her kazoo.

With that, Roxanne skipped merrily toward the milling group of marchers, anxious to assume her well-deserved place back among the elite of Kennedy High.

Chapter 9

Zack stuck a tin kazoo in his mouth and blew the highest note he could reach. An ear-splitting bleat ruptured the cool morning air, and Stacy, who was standing beside him, covered her ears.

"Yeow!" she yelled. "That's awful!"

"What? You don't like my music?" Zack asked, frowning playfully.

"Music? Is that what you call it?" Stacy teased. "I thought you were practicing your duck calls."

Zack answered her with another loud blast on his kazoo.

Stacy shook her fist at him, "You're asking for it, McGraw!" Then she reached over and pulled his visor down over his eyes.

Zack had surprised Stacy by bringing her a white visor with battery-operated little red and blue lights. He'd brought one for himself, too, and for the first hour of that morning they had gone around grinning fiendishly and blinking their visors at anyone who would watch.

Zack made a move to tickle her, but Jonathan Preston's voice interrupted them.

"March Right!" Jonathan shouted, cupping his hands around his mouth. His voice was starting to get a little hoarse, which amused the already-giddy marchers no end.

"Hey, froggy! We already did that one!" Daniel Tackett shouted. He was standing off to Stacy and Zack's left.

"Is that you, Tackett?" Jonathan shouted, shielding his eyes. "There's so much glare I can barely see you."

Daniel was wearing a bright Hawaiian shirt that was two sizes two big for him, and over that he had draped five very loud ties that he'd found at a vintage clothing store. Everyone had been teasing him about his outfit all morning.

"It's me all right," Daniel called back. "And I said we've already done 'March Right'." Daniel demonstrated by dragging his left foot around, as Jonathan had shown them.

Lily peered over the top of Jonathan's shoulder with a wicked grin on her face. "Yes, but have you done 'March Wrong'?"

She sprang out from behind Jonathan's back and hopped around in a circle flopping her arms.

Stacy turned to Zack and crossed her eyes. "March Wrong! I get it!" She started staggering around, bumping into Zack and careening away, then returning to knock into him again.

Zack immediately joined her, and the other marchers spread out to give them room.

"Hey, you guys should start an act. You look great together," Pamela shouted from the far side of the circle.

"Laurel and Hardy they're not!" Eric cracked.

Zack and Stacy were giggling so hard they nearly missed Jonathan's next order.

"Grab your partner, 'round and 'round," Jonathan shouted in his best square-dance-caller voice. "March them up, and march them down!"

Zack stopped laughing long enough to loop his arm through Stacy's. They skipped in a circle, giggling insanely. Then Zack placed his strong hands firmly on her waist and, in one smooth move, lifted the tiny gymnast up high over his head.

Stacy let out a shriek of delight. The sky was a vibrant blue above her, the air crisp and clear, and it seemed she couldn't be happier. When Zack placed her back on the ground lightly, her face was flushed with exhilaration.

"Zack, I've got an idea!" she said, her eyes sparkling as she looked up at him. "That reminded me of the team tumbling we used to do at the YMCA."

"Team tumbling?" he repeated, a bemused twinkle in his eye. "I thought you were strictly solo."

Something in the tone of his voice made Stacy realize he wasn't just talking about gymnastics. Slowly she answered, "Solo is good, most of the time, but if you find the right partner — " She paused for an instant, then said exuberantly, "It can be really fun! Come on, I'll show you."

Zack stepped back, his hands held up in protest. "Nothing airborne for me, thanks. No way are you going to get *me* doing flips. I can run and lift, but that's — "

"That's all you have to do," Stacy broke in, her voice ringing with excitement. "I'll do the flips and walkovers as we march along."

The prospect of performing with Zack sounded better and better by the minute. She paced in a tight circle, frantically trying to remember some of her old gymnastic routines. Then she stopped and cocked her head up at Zack, who was watching her patiently.

"Zack, do you think you could lift me and march with me on your shoulder?"

"Are you kidding?" He instantly scooped her up in his arms. "Piece of cake!"

Before she knew it, Stacy found herself cradled in Zack's arms and staring directly into his enormous blue eyes. They were so close their lips almost touched.

"Maybe you, uh, could carry me on your shoulder for part of the route," she said, not taking her eyes away from his. "Then I could do some flips during the solo part."

"I think I'd like that," Zack answered, his voice a husky rumble in his throat. He didn't put her back down but hugged her ever so slightly to him.

All around them, kids from Kennedy High were coming up with wackier and wackier ideas for the free-form part of the marching, but Zack and Stacy didn't move. They seemed to be frozen in time.

"Attention everybody!" Brenda Austin's voice cut through the confusion. She was standing in the back of Matt's truck, waving her arms to get their attention. "Is everybody ready?"

A cheer went up around them, and Zack reluctantly set Stacy down. Then they joined the others in pulling out their kazoos and blasting out as loud as possible.

"I take that as a definitive yes!" Brenda responded from her perch above them on the truck.

Everyone laughed and Zack slipped his arm around Stacy's waist. She leaned her head against his shoulder. The warm smell of his shirt made her dizzy with anticipation.

"Now, in fifteen minutes," Brenda instructed, "we're going to roll down to the corner and take our position in line for the judging. We'll all pose, smiling our best, and the judges will decide who gets the blue ribbon." She winked broadly and added, "Which will, of course, be Garfield House!"

Another exuberant blast from several dozen kazoos answered her, and she waved her hands for silence one last time. "It is now exactly nine-forty AM," Brenda said. "Take a break, and I'll see you all back here at nine-fifty sharp!"

There was a loud burst of cheering, then the marchers began to mill around. Some headed for the lawn to sit down, and others just stood in groups chatting.

"I'll tell you one thing," Zack said, rubbing his stomach, "all this marching practice has made me hungry. Why don't I run to the corner and pick us up some doughnuts?"

"Great idea," Stacy said, nodding her approval. "That'll give me a chance to talk to

Jonathan and Lily about our new tumbling act."

Stacy watched Zack jog off down the block and felt a little shiver of delight run down her back. They were really hitting it off, and it felt wonderful. She suddenly spotted Jonathan's familiar Indiana Jones hat bobbing above the crowd and eagerly raced to talk to him.

As soon as Brad Davidson slid out of his car across the street from Garfield House, he spotted Brenda's familiar silhouette, standing on the back of Matt Jacobs's pickup. She was carrying her clipboard and a pen, giving last-minute instructions to her various helpers. Brad, with a huge smile on his face, strode confidently across the road. Maybe now we'll have a chance to talk, he thought to himself.

"Brad, you made it!" Brenda greeted him with a warm smile.

"Looks like you've got everything under control," he said, hopping up to join her on the truck.

Brenda nodded happily, then looked down at her clipboard. "The marchers are all taking a short break. Then everyone has to go over to the judges' pavilion."

"How about a cup of coffee?" Brad said. "I'd really love to talk to you."

Brenda smiled vaguely at him, then suddenly shouted, "No, Tim, that banner has to drape across the hood from left to right. You're putting it on backward!"

A skinny teen in cut-offs and loafers stepped back from the banner he was taping into place, realized his mistake, and flashed an "okay" sign back at Brenda.

"I'm sorry, Brad, what'd you say?" Brenda asked distractedly, turning back to him.

"I'd really like to talk to you," Brad said, lowering his voice. "I thought maybe you could spare me a few minutes."

"Oh, hey, Brad, not now! I've got a million things to take care of." Brenda glanced down at her watch. "And only ten minutes to do it in."

Brad shrugged. "I was hoping we could — "

They were suddenly blasted with sound from the speakers placed on either side of the pickup, and Brenda covered her ears. "No, Alex!" she shouted. "That sound level is just too loud. The marchers will never hear their instructions."

Lily Rorshack raced up to the truck and called, "Brenda, Pamela needs you at the back to check the final banner positions."

"Be right there!" Brenda tucked her clipboard under one arm and moved to jump off the bed of the truck. Brad grabbed her arm in desperation.

"Brad, please, I'm busy," Brenda said, jerking her arm away. As she leaped off the back of the truck, she called over her shoulder, "Some other time, okay?"

"Fine!" Brad spat the word out after her, then angrily kicked the side of the pickup. Brenda's indifference to him and his problems made things a hundred times worse. How could she just shut him out like that?

Brad jumped off the float and crashed directly into a girl trying to make her way through the crowd.

They both let out an *"Ooomph!"* and Brad stepped back to see if she was all right. It was the gymnast he'd bumped into at the sub shop the week before.

"Well, if it isn't the discus thrower," he said with a wry grin. "Hope I didn't shake you up too much."

Stacy recognized Brad and greeted him with a dazzling smile. "Well, if it isn't one of Kennedy High's favorite alumni," she said, coming on strong. "It's great to see you!"

Brad was a little surprised by the warm reception he was getting. His spirits immediately perked up, and he thought, This'll show Brenda. Who needs her, anyway?

"You know, we're going to have to stop running into each other like this," Brad said, pouring on the famous Davidson megawatt charm. Stacy's infectious laugh bubbled up in reply, and Brad grinned with pleasure. "Boy, you sure are a kick! What's up?"

Stacy thrust her arms up in the air and sang out, "The sky! The clouds! And me!" Then, to Brad's stunned surprise, she did a back handspring from a standing position. Stacy could never resist a little harmless flirting. Guys loved it, and it made her feel pretty good, too; Stacy craved lots of attention.

For the first time in a long time, Brad found himself laughing, loud and hard. He also noticed for the first time just how cute Stacy was. Maybe she was just what the doctor ordered, he thought, looking over in Brenda's direction to see if she was watching.

Clutching Brad's arm excitedly, Stacy burbled, "This parade is going to be fantastic! We're all doing wacky march steps, and I'm going to do a trick I haven't thought about in years. Want to see it?"

"Sure!" Brad replied with a laugh.

"Well, you'll have to help out," Stacy said, taking hold of his hands. "You see, it's a team trick."

"Just tell me what to do," Brad said good-naturedly.

Stacy spotted Jonathan standing a few feet away and mouthed at him, "Watch!" He nodded and stopped what he was doing. Stacy, still clutching Brad's hands, leaned in close to him and instructed, "On the count of three, swing your hands above your head and I'll hop up onto your shoulder. Oh, they're going to love this!"

Zack had practically flown all the way to the coffee shop and back. Now he was holding a bag of glazed doughnuts in his teeth, trying his best not to spill too much of the hot coffee steaming from the two cups he was also carrying. A huge grin was plastered across his face. He and Stacy were really on the same wavelength. As he rounded the corner by Garfield House, Zack shook his head and chuckled. How could he ever have doubted that things wouldn't work out?

"Three!" Zack heard Stacy shout in a raspy voice over the noise of the rest of the crowd. He looked up just in time to catch her hopping onto a tall, dark-haired guy's shoulder. Then she clapped her hands, leaped up off the stranger's shoulders into a midair split, and landed securely in his arms. Everyone applauded, especially Jonathan, who shouted, "Bravo! Let's use it, okay?"

Zack stood there, absolutely stunned, and watched Stacy hop lightly out of the boy's arms and congratulate him with a hug. He couldn't understand it. What was Stacy doing flirting with that guy like that?

For a moment, Zack thought he was going to be sick. How could he have done this to himself again? For the third time, he'd made an absolute idiot of himself over a girl who obviously didn't like him as much as he *thought* she did.

His face lost all expression. "Way to go, McGraw," Zack muttered angrily to himself. "You really know how to pick 'em."

The closer he got to the float, the more his hurt turned into anger. He didn't even notice the coffee sloshing out of the cups all over the ground. When he reached Stacy, he thrust a half-filled Styrofoam cup and the bag of doughnuts into her hands.

"I see you've found a new partner for the parade," he said flatly.

"What?" Stacy's smile slid off her face as she took the bag from Zack.

"I guess he'll be meeting you at the fireworks tonight," Zack said coolly, "because I sure won't."

Stacy felt like she'd been slapped and instantly lashed back. "That's just fine with me!" she hissed at him. "I couldn't care less what you do!"

Stacy pulled her old defensive wall around her tight. What was his problem, anyway? All she was doing was being friendly to Brad, who obviously didn't know many people here. If Zack was going to be so hotheaded about it, though, then she certainly didn't need him. Without another word, she turned her back on Zack, who flushed beet-red and stomped off toward the street.

Brad watched Zack go, then looked down at Stacy. "What's going on?"

"Nothing," Stacy replied quickly. She looked up at Brad and shrugged, "Nothing important. I really wasn't interested in watching the fireworks anyway."

Over her shoulder, Brad could see Brenda busily going from person to person, checking things off her list on the clipboard. "Yeah," he muttered, "all this Fourth of July stuff is for kids."

Stacy nodded, folding her arms defiantly across her chest.

"Listen, I'm having a party tonight," Brad said slowly, his eyes still fixed on Brenda, who was taking her place among the marchers. "Nothing fancy, just some friends from Princeton. Why don't you come over early? You could help me set up for it."

Stacy bit her lip. She could see Zack's car swerve out of the parking lot and speed off down the street, away from Garfield House and away from her. Deep down, she hated to see him go. But she had to stand up for herself, too. As the car disappeared around the corner, she mumbled softly, "That sounds like a great idea. Just great."

Chapter
10

Roxanne eased the car into the parking spot of her mother's town house and switched off the ignition. With a satisfied smile, she nestled her head back against the cushy headrest.

"Fabulous!" she sighed. "Everything was perfect — just perfect!"

It was just twelve-thirty in the afternoon. The parade had come to an end only half an hour earlier, with the float from Garfield House winning the prize for Most Creative entry. Everyone was thrilled — all their hard work had paid off. To celebrate their triumph, Brenda and the gang had all agreed to meet at Billy's Ritz for lunch. Jonathan and Lily, and even Pamela, had all made a special effort to thank Roxanne for the sashes, and to include her in the festivities. She was in! After taking a moment to savor her hard-won victory, Roxanne briskly swung out of the car and danced up the walk to the town house entrance. She snapped her fingers above her head and took the stairs two at a time. Slipping her key in the deadbolt, she turned the lock and pushed open the heavy walnut door. A blast of frigid air greeted her inside.

"Anybody home?" Roxanne shouted up the stairs from the long foyer. She was answered only by the low hum of the air-conditioner. "Mom?" she called out hopefully, peering around the corner into the deserted living room. There was no reply.

On a sudden impulse, she ran into the kitchen and checked the refrigerator door. Occasionally her mother would leave a message for her under one of the magnets. There was nothing.

Roxanne leaned against the kitchen counter and listened to the clock over the stove tick quietly away in the silence. The refrigerator clicked on, the sudden noise a loud intrusion into the blanket of silence covering the Easton home.

"Some Fourth of July," Roxanne grumbled bitterly. Holidays were really a joke around her house. Other families would plan events with the express purpose of being together, while her family seemed to go to great lengths to stay apart.

The old familiar feelings of despair and loneliness started to surface and sour her mood. With a quick toss of her long red hair, Roxanne squelched the unwelcome thoughts, determined not to let anything spoil her day. Taking a deep breath, she dashed upstairs to her bedroom to change her clothes and freshen her makeup. She, Roxanne Easton, had a luncheon date to prepare for. Even if her family didn't care about her, now she had friends who did.

The thought of "friends" brought on a sharp twinge of guilt about leaving Frankie back at the Foxy Lady. Roxanne grimaced at the image of Frankie, waiting forlornly for her old friend to come back and bring her to the parade. But everything had gotten so hectic and confused. So much had been happening at once — the judging, the marching along the route. There had never been a good time to slip away. Besides, it was the first real fun Roxanne had had in a long time. She hadn't wanted to miss a minute of it.

Of course, by the time the parade ended, it was far too late to do anything about Frankie. And surely Frankie wouldn't have sat around for three whole hours waiting for her. Roxanne paused just long enough to contemplate that dire thought, her makeup brush poised in midair. Then she continued applying the pink powder. No, that was ridiculous. Sensible Frankie, realizing that Roxanne had been held up, would have gone on home.

She'd give Frankie a call before she went to lunch, Roxanne decided. Just to explain and patch things up. Frankie would understand.

Roxanne stepped back from the full-length mirror in her bedroom and examined her reflection critically. She had chosen a crisp white strapless sundress to wear for the afternoon. It gave a fresh, wholesome, All-American look to her natural beauty without making her come on too strong. Now that she was easing back into the crowd, she didn't want to press her luck by being too flamboyant or pushy.

A loud "brrrring!" snapped her out of her reverie. Still admiring herself in the mirror, Roxanne reached over and picked up the pink Princess phone on her bedstand.

"Hey, Rox? It's me — Vince!"

All the color drained out of her face at the sound of his voice. Vince! The absolute last person she wanted to talk to now. Why hadn't she left five minutes ago? She wanted to kick herself for wasting so much time admiring herself in front of the mirror.

"Oh . . . uh, hi, Vince." She tried the best she could to put some enthusiasm in her voice.

"Josh just stopped by my house and said he'd seen you at the parade," Vince continued. "Did your mom change her mind?"

"About what?" Rox answered cautiously.

"About being grounded."

"Oh, *that!*" Roxanne thought quickly, trying to cover herself. "Oh, yes, she did. Isn't that wonderful? It was such a last-minute thing," she rattled on blithely. "She thought that, since I worked so hard on the float, and since the crowd was depending on me to come through with the sashes, it wouldn't be fair to not let me go."

"That's wonderful!" Vince broke in excitedly. "Now you won't have to miss my family's picnic. They were really disappointed that they weren't going to meet you. This is great news!"

As he talked, Roxanne slumped heavily down onto the bed. She was really stuck. She couldn't turn Vince down without coming flat out and telling him why she didn't want to go to the picnic. And that would be the same as dumping him as a boyfriend — he'd take it as a personal rejection.

Besides, if she did give Vince a lame excuse, and then went out with the crowd to celebrate, and that narc Josh mentioned it to Vince later, the result would be even worse. She couldn't afford to give the crowd a reason to turn against her again — her newly won position just wasn't secure enough.

"So you can come to the picnic, right?" Vince asked, his voice jerking her back to the present.

There was no way out of it. Roxanne wouldn't be meeting the gang back in Georgetown — she would be spending the entire day at a boring backyard barbecue, with people she didn't know or even care about. It was a tragic waste.

"I'd love to," Roxanne said dully. She could hardly get the words out.

"Fantastic!" Vince's voice reverberated with delight. "I'll be over right away to pick you up."

"Great," Roxanne replied in a tiny voice. After he hung up, she sat silently on the bed, listening to the dial tone drone in her ear.

"I can't believe it!" Frankie fumed, slamming her purse against the black leather stool by the cash register. "I just can't believe it!"

She paced angrily around the main floor of the Foxy Lady, weaving in and out of the displays, kicking at the racks in frustration. The red clock above the door read 12:45. Over three hours had slowly ticked by since Roxanne had dashed out of the store, promising to return in a few minutes. Three agonizingly long hours, enough time for

Frankie to work up a towering rage.

She hadn't wasted her time alone, either. The last two hours had been spent refining the blistering lecture she intended to blast Roxanne with as soon as she came in the door. Roxanne's failure to come back and get Frankie was only the beginning. Frankie intended to let her so-called friend have it, once and for all, for every lousy, awful thing she had ever done over all the years they had known each other.

"This is *ridiculous*." Frankie looked up at the clock again, then picked up a copy of *Elle* magazine that was lying on one of the black-and-white couches, and thumbed through it restlessly. She had waited this long to tell Roxanne off, she could wait a few minutes longer.

When the clock chimed at one o'clock, Frankie threw down the magazine and decided to face facts. Roxanne had no intention of coming back to get her. She was a stupid idiot to have expected any shred of decency from Ms. Rox Easton. It was time to give up and go home.

"The only person worse than Roxanne," she growled at her reflection in one of the mirrors, "is you, for letting her do this to you over and over and over again!"

Suddenly she heard the sound of someone tapping on the glass window by the front door. At last! Frankie spun on her heel, gathering the full force of her anger inside.

But instead of Roxanne, she saw two strange women peering in at her, gesturing for her to open the door.

"We're closed!" she mouthed at them.

The two ladies conferred with each other, then the shorter one with the big straw hat asked, "Why?"

Frankie's anger was at the boiling point as she moved to the door, pointed at the "Please come again" sign and shouted, "It's the Fourth of July — this is a holiday!"

The tall lady with the big dark sunglasses huffed, "Well, if this is a holiday and you're closed, what are *you* doing here?"

Frankie crossed her arms and tilted her head. "Good question."

With that she turned and marched over to the leather stool where she'd put her purse, pausing just long enough to kick at a mannequin.

Another knock sounded on the glass, and she shouted over her shoulder, "We're closed! Come back Monday."

"Aw, come on, let us in," a familiar voice pleaded.

Frankie turned and was greeted with the sight of three smiling faces pressed up against the glass.

"Josh!" Frankie's scowl changed to a smile. Beside her boyfriend stood Pamela and Eric, both waving crazily and laughing. Frankie rushed to unlock the glass door and let them in.

"It's lunchtime," Josh announced, leaping through the doorway and giving Frankie a huge bear hug, "and you are to be my guest of honor at Billy's Ritz. I missed you!"

"The whole crowd's meeting there in exactly five minutes," Eric announced as he pointed to his watch. "To officially celebrate Garfield House's winning entry in the parade."

"Oh, did we win something?" Frankie said, momentarily forgetting Roxanne in her happiness for the group's work. "That's great!"

"All that marching's made me starved," Pamela called from one of the dress racks. She held one of the sequined designer originals up against her overalls and struck a model's pose. "How do I look?"

"It's you!" Eric joked. "Buy it."

"Frankie, the parade was an absolute blast!" Josh went on, grabbing one of the hats from a sleek mannequin and setting it on his head. "I wish you could've been there."

"Somebody had to clean up the shop," Frankie replied, trying to control her anger.

"Yeah, Rox told us you volunteered to do it, since she made the sashes," Pamela said. "That's how we knew where you'd be. It was really nice of you to forfeit the parade to clean up."

"She said that?" Frankie could hardly believe her ears.

"Those sashes made a big difference, too," Eric added. "The marchers really looked like a unit with them on."

Frankie took a deep breath, trying desperately to stay calm. This all seemed like something out of a bad dream. She moved silently to the front door. The others followed her outside.

"You know, I think we might have misjudged Roxanne," Eric said as they walked down the sidewalk toward Pamela's car.

"I think you're right," Pamela agreed. "Look at all the time she put into sewing the sashes. It was really a generous gesture on her part."

"Vince is always saying we should give her another chance," Josh added, looking over at Frankie.

"Yeah. I mean, she didn't know until the last minute that we'd include her in the parade," Eric went on. "She wasn't expecting to get anything out of it at all."

Frankie stopped in mid-stride and let out a yowl of frustration. "That does it! I think I've heard about as much as I can stand!"

Eric and Pamela were completely shocked by her sudden outburst, and their mouths hung open in dismay.

"What's the matter?" Josh asked, his brow knit with concern.

Frankie groped for words to explain herself and her feelings. All at once, she realized she was taking out her frustration on the wrong people. It wasn't their fault that she had let Roxanne use her — again.

"Listen, you guys," Frankie said quietly, "why don't you go on to lunch without me?"

"Aw, come on, Frankie," Josh said, lightly touching her arm.

"No, please, I've got this rotten headache." Frankie pressed her fingers to her temples. "I'm in such a lousy mood, I'd ruin everybody's time." She managed to force out a weak smile. "I think I'd better go home and regroup."

"Want me to come with you?" Josh asked, peering into her downcast eyes.

Frankie shook her head. "I think I'd better be alone. Right now, I'm not fit to be around other people."

Josh pulled her over to the edge of the sidewalk and looked into her face searchingly. "Did I do something wrong?"

"No, of course not." Frankie reached up and patted his cheek. "I'll meet you later for the fireworks and explain then, okay?"

"If that's what you want." Josh still wasn't convinced.

"It's what I want." To reassure him, Frankie brushed his lips with a kiss.

He squeezed her shoulder, then jogged off to join Pamela and Eric.

"Frankie said she'd join us for the big fireworks finale tonight," he announced. "For now, though, I have been instructed to eat her share of lunch."

Pamela looked over at Frankie uncertainly and called, "You sure you're okay?"

"You guys go on," Frankie replied. "I'm fine, really. I just need to go home and lie down. See you tonight!"

"Folks, you heard it from the horse's mouth," Josh said, stepping between Eric and Pamela and looping one arm through each of theirs. "On to Billy's Ritz!"

Frankie longed to run after them and join the crowd down at the restaurant. But what if Roxanne was there? Frankie didn't think she'd be able to stop herself from blowing up at her in front of everyone. Swinging her straw bag over her shoulder, she turned and headed straight for the nearest bus stop. What she had to say to Roxanne was between the two of them, and the two of them alone.

Chapter
11

Vince pulled his Blazer over to the curb, set the brake, then dashed around to the passenger side. He swung the door open and, smiling broadly, gestured up at the house behind him. "This is it. We're here."

Roxanne stepped gingerly onto the sidewalk and looked up at the house. It was a fairly typical suburban home, a rambling ranch-style house that sprawled across a low, tree-covered hill. Roxanne had to admit, she hadn't expected Vince's house to look so normal, or so pleasant. Shrugging her shoulders, she started to walk toward the front door.

Before she'd gone more than a foot, Vince grabbed her hand and pulled Roxanne toward the side of the house. "Let's go in through the arbor. It's prettier," he explained. "Everyone's out back, anyway."

Roxanne nodded curtly. Feeling every bit the

martyr, she walked beside Vince through the shady grove toward a large wrought-iron gate. A rich confusion of voices and music, punctuated by shouts of laughter and the high-pitched squeals of children, drifted over to them from the direction of the backyard.

This is going to be just as bad as I imagined, Roxanne thought, setting her teeth grimly in preparation for the crush of family members she'd have to face in just a few short moments.

Suddenly, the bushes around them exploded with movement and Vince was tackled by three little boys, who tried with all their might to wrestle him to the ground.

"Help! Help! I'm being attacked by bandits," he yelled, halfheartedly trying to resist their efforts. Roxanne leaped out the way, hoping their horsing around hadn't gotten any dirt on her dress.

"Come on, Uncle Vince, give up!" one of the boys shouted.

"Yeah, we got you covered!" another one of his assailants piped up.

"Give up? Never!" Vince bellowed, standing up abruptly, the three boys clinging to his arms. He took two of the giggling, squirming boys and pinioned them under his arms. The third he held by the shirt collar. The boys were laughing too hard to struggle free. Vince turned to Roxanne, his eyes gleaming with mischief, and said, "What do you think I should do with these clowns?"

Roxanne stood there, speechless. Then she realized that this was a game Vince had played with these kids before because, without waiting for her answer, he said, "Dump them in the garbage? Drop them off the roof?"

There was a chorus of anguished pleas for mercy. Vince let them go all at once, and the boys tumbled to the soft, mossy ground in an unceremonious clump.

"Hey, guys," he said, "listen up. I want you to meet someone special."

The boys noticed Roxanne for the first time and scrambled to their feet. Standing side by side, they formed a sort of ladder — each one was a little taller than the next. They were all wearing their best Sunday clothes, which were covered with dirt and grime. Each boy's thick, dark hair was a mess, peppered with leaves and bits of grass.

"Roxanne, meet my brother, Tony," Vince said, standing behind the tallest boy, who nodded politely. "And my youngest brother, Little Sal," Vince pointed to the next tousle-head in line.

The boy stared at Roxanne in openmouthed awe. Vince nudged him gently, and the kid came to his senses. "Gosh, you're beautiful!" he said.

"Come off it, Sal," Vince said, winking at Roxanne as he ruffled the boy's head. "You're going to embarrass the lady!"

"Well, it's true," the last boy piped up. He stepped forward and said confidently, "Hi, I'm Patrick DeSantis, Vince's nephew." The boy, who couldn't have been more than ten, swaggered over to Roxanne with practiced ease. "Look, you going to be busy later? Maybe we can have a dance or something."

"You, I'm going to kill!" Vince grabbed Patrick

by the back of his pants and yanked him into the air.

"I was just kidding, Uncle Vince," Patrick squealed. "Really, I was! No offense, lady!"

Just then the gate swung open and a slender, strikingly beautiful woman looked out to see what all the commotion was about.

"Vincent! You're finally here," she cried, stepping gracefully across the lawn toward him. "We thought you'd gotten hit by a car or something!"

Vince dropped Patrick and the three boys scampered off through the trees. "Hi, Mom," Vince said. "I want you to meet Roxanne!"

Roxanne couldn't believe her eyes. This stunning woman was actually Vince's mother? She was smartly dressed in a gauzy summer dress in gold-colored raw silk, her honey-blonde hair pulled up neatly in a style even Roxanne's mother would have envied.

"Um, I uh — oh, hello, Mrs. DiMase," Roxanne blurted out unceremoniously. Vince's mother smiled and embraced her warmly. Mrs. DiMase was almost as tall as Roxanne, and the scent of her perfume was subtle and delicate.

"It's lovely to meet you," the older woman said. "Please, just call me Leona. All my friends do." Mrs. DiMase put her arm around Roxanne's shoulder and, turning to Vince, said, "I'll introduce Roxanne to the family. You go put on a clean shirt. You look like a hurricane hit you."

Vince looked down at the maroon polo shirt he was wearing. His little tumble with the boys had left him a few souvenir smudges of dirt across his chest. "Sure, Mom," he said agreeably. "Look, Rox, I'll be back in a minute."

Roxanne barely heard him. Mrs. DiMase had already swept her into the backyard to join the rest of the gathering. Within five minutes she had met seven aunts, five uncles, two sets of grandparents, and uncounted nephews and nieces, not to mention countless other people who were just good friends of the family. Everyone seemed to be talking at once and nobody seemed to be listening to what anyone else was saying. More important, nobody seemed to care. They were having too good a time.

The landscaping in the backyard cleverly created little pockets of green grass surrounded by bushes and flowering shrubs, where tables and chairs had been arranged so people could sit and chat. A lavish buffet table was set up on the patio and was covered by a red, green, and white awning. The array of food was endless. There were, of course, huge platters of pasta, with different sauces in tureens alongside. Heaping bowls of freshly grated Parmesan and Romano cheeses, dotted the long table, with several green salads and bowls of fresh fruit clustered at the far end next to long, skinny loaves of Italian bread.

"You must be hungry," Mrs. DiMase said, depositing a plate and some silverware into Roxanne's hands. "Have some lunch. Oh, here's Vince."

Roxanne turned to see Vince weaving his way toward them, stopping here and there to greet a friend or kiss an aged aunt on the cheek. He was wearing a pair of white pleated slacks and a pale blue shirt, open at the collar. With a start, Roxanne realized that she had rarely seen Vince dressed in anything but outdoor gear and his ever-present Baltimore Orioles cap. He looked up and caught her staring at him. His rugged features lit up with a broad smile and, quickening his pace, he soon joined her.

"Here you are!" he said, "I thought I'd lost you."

"I'll leave you two alone now," Mrs. DiMase said, patting Roxanne gently on the shoulder. "Don't forget to leave room for the gelati!"

Vince grabbed a plate and gestured toward the food. "Shall we?"

Suddenly Roxanne realized she was ravenous. They worked their way down the table, sampling different dishes, and wound up with heaping plates, which they carried to one of the picnic tables on the lawn. To Roxanne's delight, everything tasted fabulous.

"This is great!" she said to Vince as she dipped her spoon into the last of the cream sauce on her plate.

"You sound surprised," Vince said.

"To tell you the truth," she confessed, "I expected the food to be more . . . more. . . ." She shook her head and Vince laughed.

"Like something out of a pizza parlor?" he ventured.

Roxanne grinned and nodded.

"This food is northern Italian style," he explained. "It's always lighter and more subtle than the Neapolitan style." Vince grinned and added,

117

"Or so I'm told. My family originally came from Lombardy, so they're a little biased."

"Did your mom actually cook all of this?" Roxanne asked incredulously.

Vince motioned for her to lean closer to him. "I'm letting you in on a family secret," he whispered in her ear. "Mom had a lot of help; she *hates* to cook."

Roxanne's eyes widened and she exclaimed, "You're kidding!"

Vince shook his head, his eyes dancing mischievously, then added, "Just don't tell Grandma DiMase, or she'll have a fit. As far as she knows, my mother slaved alone over a hot stove for three days whipping up this feast. Needless to say, it was a family project."

Roxanne debated with herself about going back for seconds when some rousing accordion music began to play. A cheer went up from the crowd, and there was a surge of movement toward the far end of the lawn.

"That's my Uncle Paolo," Vince explained, a huge grin creasing his face. "Come on, you don't want to miss this!" He jumped up and gestured for her to follow, then disappeared into the circle of onlookers.

Reluctantly Roxanne got up and followed him. Well, the food was okay, and everyone was pretty nice, but enough was enough. Here she sat, surrounded by a bunch of strangers when she could have been having some real fun with the crowd down at Billy's Ritz in Georgetown. And now her worst nightmare was about to come true — they were going to start singing corny songs played by some old geezer on a screechy accordion.

Everyone had formed a semicircle around Uncle Paolo, a slim man of about fifty, dressed in a light gray summer suit. With his dark hair graying slightly at the temples, he looked more like the chairman of some big corporation than a musician. His fingers were flying across the keyboard as he played a rousing tarantella. Within seconds, people were clapping along in time. Vince grabbed Roxanne and said, "Come on, let's dance."

"Vince!" Roxanne moaned. "Please, I don't know how to dance to this kind of music." The thought of making a spectacle of herself in front of everybody made her want to sink into the ground and die.

"But I do," he countered. "I'll teach you." Before she could refuse, he grabbed her around the waist and spun her out among the other couples.

Roxanne was greeted with another surprise. Half-expecting to get her new sandals massacred by Vince and his clumsy feet, she was stunned to discover that he not only knew how to dance, but made her look good in the process.

"Where did you learn to dance like this?" she asked in astonishment.

"Are you kidding? I'm Italian," he replied with a grin. "We learn to dance before we learn to walk." He spun her around and around, and Roxanne found she had to concentrate totally to keep up with him.

Uncle Paolo segued into a new tune, and the dancers fell into a long, boisterous line.

A pudgy older man grabbed Roxanne's hand. "Come on," he called, "it's the line dance."

Vince jogged to catch up with her, finally taking her other hand. He whispered in her ear, "You are holding the hand of one of the most important men in Congress."

Roxanne turned to look at the man who was skipping along, singing at the top of his lungs, and giggled back. "You're kidding!"

"He is also an authority on the polka, the waltz, and various forms of line dances." This time Vince had to shout to be heard over the music and the senator's singing.

By now everybody was on the floor — kids, grandparents, aunts, and uncles — all snaking their way around the tables and chairs, laughing as they went.

Tune followed tune. Roxanne found herself in great demand as a partner, as one after another of the men in the family asked her to dance. At first she felt terribly self-conscious, afraid they might laugh at her. But everyone was charming and unpretentious — they simply wanted to enjoy the day's festivities. Their merriment was infectious and hard to resist.

Then little Patrick appeared at her arm and stiffly asked her to dance. He was so formal about it, and Roxanne couldn't help smiling as he walked her out onto the floor, looking very dignified and adult. He barely came up to her waist, and as they waltzed to Paolo's music, Roxanne realized how incredibly silly they must look together.

Then a very unexpected and weird realization came over her. She didn't care. For the very first time in her life, Roxanne didn't feel she had to impress anyone. She just had to be herself. Vince's family had all accepted her the way she was.

As the waltz ended, Vince returned to her side and, leaning down close to her ear, whispered, "Having a good time?"

She looked up at him, her eyes shining with happiness, and said, "The time of my life!"

Chapter
12

"Should I put these chips on the table?" Stacy called to Brad from the big tree-lined patio of the Davidson house.

"Thanks, Stacy," Brad yelled back through the kitchen door. "That would be great."

Stacy popped open the plastic bags and poured the chips into the purple-and-white striped bowls, then placed a bowl at each end of the table. The patio furniture had been moved onto the lawn and two long folding tables sat in their place in front of the sliding glass doors. Brad had thrown matching tablecloths across them and stacked up purple plastic plates, with matching napkins, forks, and spoons. A pair of speaker columns was propped up on orange crates at either side of the house.

Strings of Japanese paper lanterns stretched above the patio across the lawn to the pool, where two circular tables with yellow umbrellas held large coolers full of iced cans of soda. Stacy took it all in as she idly nibbled on one of the rippled potato chips.

What am I doing here? she suddenly asked herself. Brad had wanted her to help him set up, but there had been little to do. All of the hors d'oeuvres had been ordered from Earthly Delights, one of the best caterers in Rose Hill. Brad hadn't spared any expense on this little backyard get-together.

The only thing left to do was greet the guests. The thought of guests gave Stacy butterflies. She barely knew Brad, or his guests — old friends who'd graduated from Kennedy High before she'd arrived, and college friends from Princeton. She was certain not to know or have much in common with any of them. Suddenly Stacy felt awfully young and unsure of herself.

Brad slid one of the glass doors back and stepped out onto the patio. He held two bowls of hot buttered popcorn and, handing them to Stacy, said, "Here, put these on the table next to the chips, will you? I've got to check the spareribs."

Stacy did as she was told. Brad picked up a white cordless telephone and, crossing the patio to the large grill that held the smoking ribs, placed it on a chair nearby.

Stacy couldn't think of anything else to do to get the place ready, so she followed him over. She watched him pick up a bowl of barbecue sauce and smear the thick liquid over the cooking meat.

"Stacy, have you given much thought to what

you're going to do?" Brad asked suddenly. She looked up at him in surprise. "After you get out of high school, I mean," Brad explained.

"Not much." Stacy giggled and added, "I have enough trouble thinking about what I'm going to do next week, much less two years from now."

Brad nodded absently. "When I was in high school, everything seemed crystal clear." There was a faraway tone in his voice, and for a second Stacy had the feeling he didn't even know she was there.

"I knew exactly how my life would turn out. I was so *sure* about everything." He shook his head with annoyance. "Now, everything is blurry, like the windshield suddenly fogged up."

Stacy watched Brad closely as he rambled on, lost in his own problems. She analyzed his profile as if she were looking at a photograph. Brad was definitely handsome — tall, tan, with nice thick brown hair, and deep brown eyes. The little chip in his front tooth only added a little character to what otherwise would have been a perfect smile. In his pleated twill pants, olive-green shirt, and white linen sports jacket, he looked like a model for *GQ*. Stacy knew that lots of girls would probably fall for him at first sight, but somehow she didn't feel a thing.

In fact, she had to force herself to pay attention to what he was saying. What was she doing here? Why did she act so stubbornly at the parade? Visions of Zack kept popping into her head. She could see his crystal-blue eyes, full of humor, as he'd held her up in his arms that morning. She also saw the look of wounded pride he'd given her before walking away from the parade.

Stacy squeezed her eyes shut, trying to rid her mind of Zack's face. But the more she tried to get him out of her head, the more she ached to see him again . . . but had she blown her chances with him for the last time? Stacy opened her eyes wide and forced herself to concentrate on what Brad was saying.

"Basically, the problem is," he said with a shrug, "college just hasn't lived up to my expectations. I thought it would give me the big answers, and all I'm discovering are bigger questions."

Stacy nodded, trying to look understanding. Inside her head, a voice kept saying, "I don't belong here. What do I know about college? This party's going to be way over my head."

To her great relief the cordless phone rang, interrupting their conversation. Brad pushed up the antenna and, holding the receiver to his ear, said, "Hello?"

"Brenda!" Brad sounded like a heavy weight had been lifted off his shoulders. "I'm so glad you called!"

He leaned forward. "Hey, don't worry about it. You weren't rude. It was all my fault, anyway, for trying to talk to you then." He laughed and added, "That's the old Davidson bad timing!"

They talked for a few more minutes, and Stacy felt more and more uncomfortable.

"Absolutely! I'll have the welcome wagon meet you at the curb. See ya. 'Bye."

Brad set down the phone and turned to Stacy

with a grin. "It's going to be a great party!" He did a drum roll with his hands on the edge of a table and then returned to the grill, humming under his breath as he brushed the ribs with new energy.

He's happy because Brenda's coming over, Stacy thought. He docsn't carc if I'm here or not.

The realization didn't make her feel angry with Brad. Instead, Stacy suddenly felt disgusted with herself. She'd been flirting a guy who meant nothing to her and acting awful to the one boy she really cared about.

In that instant, Stacy realized what she had to do. She smoothed the tablecloth on the table one last time, then walked toward Brad, who was whistling merrily to himself.

"Brad?"

He looked up at her, and Stacy said simply, "Thanks for the invitation, but I really can't stay." He raised his eyebrows in confusion and she explained, "My friends are all going to be at the fireworks tonight. I think I'd like to be there with them."

Brad looked at her steadily for a moment. Then a look that hadn't been there all evening filled his eyes and he nodded, a warm smile on his face. "I think I understand." He took her hand and squeezed it gently. "Good luck to you, Stacy."

"And to you, too, Brad."

Stacy realized she meant it. She hoped it would work out for him and Brenda.

On the curb outside the house, Stacy hesitated for just a moment. Then she swallowed hard and started resolutely in the direction of Rose Hill Park. As she walked, a little prayer formed in her heart. "Please, let Zack be there!"

She was finally ready to open up to him — if he would still give her the chance.

In the afternoon sun, Vince's backyard had become dappled with light that filtered through the branches of the trees. Only the younger guests continued to dance, Vince and Roxanne among them. The older ones were sitting in chaises and lawn chairs, relaxing and watching the fun more comfortably.

A wonderful feeling of contentment washed over Roxanne. She was tired, but it was the kind of exhaustion you feel when you've enjoyed yourself completely. As she danced with Vince, she leaned her cheek against his broad chest. He pulled her closer, and they swayed slowly back and forth in time to the ballad Uncle Paolo was playing.

Suddenly, Uncle Paolo changed the tempo, and the guests recognized the tune he was playing and burst into applause. Uncle Paolo had a mischievous grin on his face as he played a long introduction. People were gesturing toward Mrs. DiMase, who was standing next to Vince's father, a tall, dark-haired man with a dazzling smile.

"Come on, Marcello," Uncle Paolo cried out. "Don't hold back. It's time for your big number with Leona."

Mr. DiMase shook his head and yelled back, "Another time. Can't you see I'm busy talking to the most beautiful girl in the world?" He wrapped his arm around his wife and cracked, "If I'm lucky, maybe she'll marry me."

There was a round of laughter, and Mrs. DiMase blushed at the compliment. Meanwhile, the other relatives crowded around the couple, pushing them toward the center of the lawn, not taking no for a answer. Finally they relented and the handsome pair swept gracefully out onto the lawn.

Roxanne caught her breath with wonder. They were dancing a tango, a gorgeous dance full of subtle, complex dips and turns. It had to be difficult to learn, but Vince's parents made it all look easy. They obviously loved dancing together. Mrs. DiMase's eyes shone with pleasure as her husband whirled her around and around. It was hard to believe they had been married for twenty years. From the adoring look on his face, Roxanne would have thought they had only just fallen in love.

"They still love each other," she whispered under her breath.

"Yeah," Vince whispered beside her. "They do." The pride in his voice as he watched his parents dance was so obvious that Roxanne felt a sharp twinge of envy. She wondered if her mother and father had ever been so in love. It was impossible for her to imagine.

"It can't last," she said bitterly. "Nothing lasts forever."

"Let me tell you something," Vince said softly, pointing toward his father. "See the flower in his lapel?"

Roxanne nodded. A tiny white rose was pinned on the lapel of his suit.

"My mother chooses a flower for him to wear, every day," Vince continued. "He never knows what kind it's going to be. It's always a surprise. And every day, my father brings my mother her breakfast in bed. Every single day of the year."

"That's so corny and old-fashioned," Roxanne said, wistfully, "and wonderful."

"Yeah, isn't it?" Vince said.

The music ended and Roxanne applauded along with the others as Mr. and Mrs. DiMase took a deep bow and returned to their friends. Vince nuzzled Roxanne's hair with his chin and whispered, "Take a walk?"

Roxanne nodded. He put his arm around her waist and they slipped into the grove, just out of sight of the other guests. A delicious woody scent suddenly filled the air and Roxanne breathed it all in luxuriously.

"You see how the sun looks so golden from here?" Vince's voice was low and husky. "This is one of my favorite spots."

Overwhelmed by the beauty of the fiery sun, Roxanne didn't trust herself to speak. She felt as if she were wrapped in a dreamy pink cloud and the slightest whisper might break the spell.

Vince seemed to feel it, too, and for the longest time they stood watching the sun melt into liquid gold across the horizon. As the last rays disappeared behind the hill, Roxanne slowly turned her face up to Vince. Their lips met in a sweet, gentle kiss, and Vince wrapped her in his arms.

As they held each other, a flood of new

emotions stirred Roxanne to the very core of her being. At first she was confused and frightened. Then, in a blinding flash, Roxanne understood what was happening to her.

For the first time in her life, she was falling in love — with Vince. And for once in her life she didn't know how to react. This new, strange, and powerful feeling was completely beyond her control. Without warning, her eyes welled up with tears.

"What's the matter?" Vince said, his brow furrowed with concern. "Are you okay? Did I say something wrong?"

Roxanne shook her head, too overwhelmed to answer. "It's nothing," she managed to gasp out. "I just — oh, Vince, I don't know. . . ." Two large tears trickled down her cheeks as Roxanne groped for the words to explain her feelings. Finally she said lamely, "There's something in my eye."

All at once she felt like a complete phony. When they first met, she had pretended to cry when she really had something in her eye, just to get his sympathy. Now Roxanne found herself pretending the same thing because she didn't know how to tell him she loved him. A great heart-wrenching sob wracked her body, and she buried her head in his chest.

Vince wrapped his arms tighter around her and held her close, stroking her hair gently with his hand. Each caress seemed to cover her with a thick blanket of trust and love.

"I'm sorry," Roxanne whispered through her tears. "I'm so sorry!"

"For what?" Vince asked gently. "For being the girl I'm crazy about?"

"Oh, Vince, I feel so happy, and so awful all at once," Roxanne sobbed. "Your family, and your parents — they're all so wonderful! You all love each other so much."

Another sob shook her and she lost control of her voice. Vince cupped her face in his strong hands, gently brushing the tears away with his thumbs, then kissed her cheek.

"Maybe that's why you're so sweet and generous." She dabbed at her eyes with her hands. "And why I've always been the way I've been. I never learned how to care, to really *care* for anyone — until now."

Vince answered her with a gentle kiss on the forehead. She smiled up at him weakly. "I look like a mess, huh?"

"You look beautiful to me." He beamed down at her with amused affection, and suddenly Roxanne was overcome with a giddy, rapturous feeling of joy. She wrapped her arms around his neck and hugged him for all she was worth.

"I'll make it up to you, Vince, I promise," Roxanne vowed, with all her heart. "To you, and everyone else."

Suddenly the image of Frankie filled her mind, and Roxanne was seized by a horrible, all-consuming guilt. For years, Frankie had been her loyal friend, faithful and ever-trusting. And Roxanne had repeatedly broken and abused that trust, manipulating their friendship until even Frankie couldn't stand it anymore. Roxanne had driven her one true friend away.

Roxanne bit her lip at the thought of Frankie, waiting back at the shop while Roxanne was off claiming the credit for the sashes with the crowd. How could she have left Frankie alone at the Foxy Lady like that after promising to go back for her?

"I've been so selfish," she muttered softly beneath her breath.

"What's that?" Vince mumbled dreamily.

"Vince, I've done a horrible thing," Roxanne said, looking directly into his eyes. Her voice was clear and firm as she said, "I've got to go see Frankie right now. I have to apologize to her."

"But the party isn't over," Vince protested. "There's still the gelati and more dancing."

"Vince, please!" Her eyes were beginning to cloud with tears again. "I have to do this!"

He studied her face and asked quietly, "Is it really that important to you?"

Roxanne nodded, her eyes pleading with him.

"All right, then," he said. "Let's go."

They slipped out of the arbor, and soon they were driving through the streets of Rose Hill toward Frankie's house.

Chapter
13

Frankie vigorously ruffled her damp hair with a thick, fuzzy bath towel as she walked from the bathroom into her bedroom. After wasting all morning in the stuffy upstairs sweatshop at the Foxy Lady, she had indulged in a long, dreamless nap. That, combined with a cool shower afterward, had done wonders to refresh her spirits and get rid of her headache. But nothing could calm her anger at Roxanne. Just the thought of seeing her ex-friend made Frankie start to seethe inside.

She shook her pale blonde hair briskly, as if by shaking her head she could also shake off her upsetting thoughts of Roxanne. Little stray wisps clung to her forehead and cheeks. It was just starting to get dark outside, and Frankie looked out the dormer window of her bedroom. The amber street lights glowed dully in the fading dusk, and lights flickered on inside houses up and down her street. The eerie whizz of bottle rockets and the staccato pop-pop-pop of firecrackers, was now reaching full fever pitch. All of the animals in the Baker household had taken refuge under beds and in closets hours before.

Frankie took a deep breath, and moved away from the window and over to her closet. Roxanne had ruined her day, but she wasn't about to let her ruin her evening. Before long, the night sky over Rose Hill Park would explode with a dazzling display of fireworks, and Frankie would be there watching, cuddled warmly in the arms of her boyfriend Josh. With that pleasant thought firmly in mind, Frankie set about getting ready.

She knew everyone at the park would be dressed casually, but Frankie felt like dressing up a bit. Pulling a pale pink flowered Laura Ashley jumper out of her closet, Frankie held it up in front of the mirror on the closet door. The tags were still on it. Frankie smiled at her reflection in the glass and nodded. She had been saving the dress for a special occasion, and tonight was certainly going to be special.

As they bounced along in Vince's red Blazer, Roxanne could hardly contain her new happiness. Before, she would have been mortified with embarrassment if anyone had seen her in a truck, but now she waved merrily to everyone they passed on the street.

"Turn here, Vince!" He nodded and the truck eased around the corner and up Adams Way. As they drove down the tree-lined street, Roxanne realized she hadn't been on this street in at least six months. She had missed it.

"There it is," she breathed nervously. "The big white house, with the green shutters and wrap-around porch."

The street was lined with cars, and there was no place to park. "Somebody must be having a big party," Vince said with a grin. "Listen, I'll drop you off here and go find a place to park."

"Right." Roxanne slid across the torn front seat and opened the door. She stepped onto the pavement and smiled back at Vince. "Wish me luck, okay?"

"You sure you'll be all right?" he asked.

Roxanne nodded and Vince slipped the jeep into gear. As soon as he pulled away from the curb, Roxanne realized that she was really nervous and a little shy about talking to Frankie. She had always prided herself on being so confident and cool under pressure. But this was very different. So much had happened to her that day; Roxanne felt like she was a totally new person. She hoped Frankie would notice the great change in her and understand.

Walking quickly up the steps onto the Baker's front porch, Roxanne reached out to ring the doorbell, then stopped. Her hands were trembling. She took a deep breath, then pressed the button. Inside the house, a bell chimed and a dog began to bark loudly. Then Roxanne heard Frankie's voice calling, "I'll get it."

Roxanne listened anxiously as her friend's footsteps clattered down the stairs to the landing. Suddenly her heart started pounding like a jackhammer. The latch jiggled, then turned, and the door swung open. Roxanne put on her brightest smile and hoped for the best.

"Hi, Josh! You . . ." Frankie's greeting died in her throat as she recognized Roxanne. The bright smile on her face faded away to a cold expressionless mask. Roxanne's heart slid into the pit of her stomach.

They stared at each other without speaking for a moment. Finally, Roxanne broke the silence.

"Hi, Frankie," she said softly, with a tiny wave of her hand.

Frankie's entire body tensed, and Rox could tell she was trying hard to control her anger. Without opening the screen door, she demanded bluntly, "What do *you* want?"

"Who is it, Frankie?" a woman's voice called from the kitchen.

Roxanne's face lit up at the sound of Mrs. Baker's voice, and she leaned toward the screen to call hello.

"It's nobody, Mom," Frankie answered pointedly. She stepped out onto the porch and pulled the big door shut behind her. "So, what do you want?" she repeated.

The chilliness of her reception had Roxanne completely flustered, and she found herself stammering, "Uh, listen, Frankie, I — I'm sorry about this morning."

"An apology from Miss Easton?" Frankie's tightly controlled voice dripped with sarcasm. "That can only mean one thing. You must want something." She folded her arms across her chest and snapped, "Well, you've come to the wrong place!"

"Frankie, I know you must be furious with me," Roxanne began, "but I came to apologize, truly. And to see if we can be friends again."

"Friends?" Frankie's bitter laugh echoed harshly in the air. "You don't know the meaning of the word! Do you really think a simple apology is going to make up for all the hurt, all the damage you've done?"

"I know how you must feel — " Roxanne started, but Frankie cut her off in mid-sentence.

"Do you really?" Frankie demanded, unable to hold back her anger any longer. "Do you know how long I waited for you at the shop? Do you know how that felt? Do you really care? Did you *ever* care — about me or anyone else?"

"Frankie, please, you don't understand. Things have changed!"

"How many times have I heard *that* one?" Frankie spat back at her fiercely. "You'll never change. You're incapable of it. Do you know how sick I am of always doing your dirty work? Covering up for you, cleaning up the shop while *you* get all the glory. . . . Do you know how disgusted I felt when I heard you make fun of Vince to the rest of the girls at the Foxy Lady?"

"Frankie, don't talk about that." Roxanne's voice was low and urgent. "I beg you."

"No, it's way past time I talked about it. I've been quiet for too long. Vince is too nice a guy to be lied to and treated like dirt!"

"That's not how it is," Roxanne protested, a panic-stricken look on her face.

"Oh, really? Tell me another one," Frankie scoffed. "I've heard you — "

"That may have been true once," Roxanne interrupted, "but, please, I'm a different person now. Frankie, you wouldn't believe what has happened to me."

"That's true, I wouldn't." Frankie threw her arms up in exasperation. "Everything that comes out out of your mouth is a lie. You don't care about Vince — "

"How can you say that?" Roxanne shouted at her.

"I was there," Frankie yelled back. "Remember? I was there in the shop when you bragged about how you pretended to be grounded, just to get out of a date with Vince. You made him look like a fool for trusting you, laughing at his family behind his back, telling everyone you're only dating him till someone better comes along."

"That's not true!" Roxanne cried.

"Oh, come on, Roxanne, admit it! You're just using poor Vince to get back in with the crowd. He's never meant anything to you, ever. You've made that loud and clear to everyone — except Vince, of course!"

"Frankie, if you'll just listen — " Roxanne mumbled miserably. She stared at the ground, her eyes blinded with tears.

"I'm through listening to anything you've got to say," Frankie cut her off. "And I will not stand by and let you hurt Vince the way you've hurt me." Her voice caught in her throat and, biting back her own tears, she declared finally, "If you ever lie to him again, about being grounded or anything else, I'll tell him the truth about everything, and — "

Frankie abruptly cut her tirade short, and Roxanne looked up to see what was the matter. All the color had drained from Frankie's face. She was staring with horror at a point just behind Roxanne on the porch. Roxanne spun around to see what it was.

Vince stood motionless on the steps, his face drawn and white in the fading light. The lines on his face were deep and painful, as if they'd been chiseled in stone. His eyes bored into Roxanne's face.

"Vince," Roxanne whispered, her voice barely audible. Frankie watched as Vince gave Roxanne one devastated, searing look, then turned and marched down the stairs. The deep gloom swallowed him up and he was gone.

The two girls didn't move for a long time. Down the street the throaty roar of an engine penetrated the night air, closely followed by the squeal of tires on the pavement. When the sound of the jeep had disappeared into the night, only the scattered explosions of firecrackers remained.

Chapter
14

Brad held one of Brenda Austin's hands in his own and stared intently at it, lost in thought. They sat huddled quietly on the couch in the living room of his house. Outside, the speakers blared the most recent hit by Huey Lewis and the News. Every now and then there would be a loud yell, followed by a splash, as more and more of the guests went tumbling into the pool.

Brad hardly noticed the goings-on outside. His original reason for throwing the party was to have a chance to see all of his old buddies from Kennedy High and introduce them to his new friends from Princeton. But from the moment Brenda had arrived, he'd only had eyes for her. And now they had come in here to talk.

Brenda patiently waited for Brad to continue speaking. In her black miniskirt and black sleeveless denim shirt that snapped up the front, the dark-eyed beauty looked more beautiful than ever.

"I always wanted to be a doctor," Brad said, "starting as far back as I can remember. The thought of it being any other other way never occurred to me. My destiny in life was to be a doctor, a great surgeon, top man in my specialty. That was all there was to it."

Brenda nodded but remained silent.

"Now I don't know," Brad continued, rubbing his temple as he talked. "To succeed in medicine — to succeed at anything, I guess — you've got to have a fire burning inside you, driving you to your goal. Otherwise you'll never make it through the program. Passion! That's what I'm driving at. You've got to have it, or it's just not worth the effort."

He looked up at Brenda, his eyes full of anguish. "I've lost that. The passion, the drive. Somehow, over the last year. . . ." He shrugged his shoulders. "I keep thinking, I've missed something in my life. I never gave myself time to just . . . be alive, to enjoy things for their own sake, not just for where they might get me."

A crooked grin creased his face and he said, "You know what I'd like to do, more than anything?"

Brenda shook her head. "No, what?"

"It's probably silly of me, real immature," he said. "But I'd like to get on a sailboat by myself, for about six months. Sail the Inland Waterway down to Florida, or island-hop around the Caribbean. You know? And never think about anything more serious than where to drop anchor that night. Just white sand, blue water, and endless sky."

"I don't think that's silly at all. Sounds like just what the doctor ordered," Brenda answered. "Ever think of taking a leave of absence from Princeton?"

Brad nodded, a little shamefacedly. "I don't know, though," he muttered. "It seems like that would be just running away from what's bothering me, avoiding a decision."

"Brad, there's nothing wrong, nothing weak about questioning yourself," Brenda said, pressing his arm comfortingly. "In a funny way, it's how we remind ourselves that we're really human, by struggling to make these choices."

Brad didn't respond but, instead, looked up at the ceiling. "I feel so — alone, though. That's the worst part."

"Like this is only happening to you, and no one else?" Brenda asked.

Brad nodded his head.

"It's hard to believe I could have made a speech advising seniors on how to cope with college," Brad joked, an embarrassed look on his face. He was referring to his well-received address delivered at Kennedy High a year before. It was then that the two of them had first agreed to go their separate ways. "I can hardly cope with what to do next week, let alone next year."

"But that's the way you should handle your anxiety," Brenda said softly. "One week, one day, one hour at a time. Try not to worry about next year."

Brad let go of her hand and leaned back against the cushions of the couch. "I wish it were that easy," he sighed, "but it's just not for me. I have to have things planned out." He smiled ruefully. "Spontaneity has never been my strong suit."

A wry grin spread over Brenda's face. "I remember."

"How could I have been so certain about my direction in life," Brad said plaintively, "and now feel so doubtful?"

Brenda cocked her head in thought, her long dark hair draped over one shoulder. "I think everyone suffers big doubts," she said, "they just hit us all at different times."

Brad remembered back to their senior year, over a year before, when Brenda had seriously wondered if she would even be able to graduate from high school. She knew all too well how paralyzing those fears could be.

"I just hope I can get through this," Brad continued. "You know, see the light at the end of the tunnel."

"There most definitely will be a light at the end of the tunnel," Brenda said gently. "But there are going to be many more tunnels in your life." She shrugged lightly. "It's called growth. It's what makes us better people."

Brad's eyes shone with admiration. "How'd you get to be so smart?"

Brenda sank back against the cushions and laughed. "I guess I've already managed to encounter a lot of tunnels in my life, and I've discovered that there's always a way out of them."

"How can I be sure things will work out?"

"You can't," she admitted. "That's the hard part, I guess — forcing yourself to believe they will."

"This must be good practice for you — listening to all my problems," Brad said, laughing self-consciously. "It's just that, lately, I've been a little . . . unfocused."

"That's nothing to be ashamed of," Brenda said quietly.

A loud whoop from the patio, followed by a splash, signaled that another victim had been tossed into the pool. Brad and Brenda both chuckled at the sound. The door to the living room suddenly burst open and Ted Mason stuck his head in, a huge grin on his face. "Got any more towels, Brad? Chris just got sacrificed to the great Water God and she's soaking wet."

"In the hall closet," Brad replied. "Next to the bathroom."

"Right," Ted said and started back out the door. Then he paused and looked back at Brad and Brenda, sitting side by side on the couch. "You guys look awfully cozy in here," he said, arching his eyebrows and grinning. "Kind of like old times."

"Go on, get out of here!" Brad cracked, picking up a pillow from the couch and firing it toward the door. "We're just talking, that's all."

Ted ducked as the pillow sailed past his head into the hall. "Sure, I understand," he said, his eyes glinting with mischief. Then he winked and added, "Don't worry, discretion is my middle name."

"Ted, go dry my sister off, before she gets

pneumonia. Now!" Brenda commanded, laughing heartily. Ted bowed and disappeared, shutting the door behind him.

"That's all we need," she said lightheartedly, "rumors that we're back together."

"Would that be so awful?" Brad asked quietly.

Brenda looked up at him in astonishment. "What do you mean?"

Brad leaned forward and, clutching her hand, said, "Listen, Bren, I knew a lot has happened over the past year, but I haven't been able to get you out of my head."

"I think about you a lot, too," Brenda said carefully. "My time with you will always be a very dear, very special memory."

"But why does it have to be a memory?" Brad ran his hand through his thick hair in frustration. "I mean, we've both changed, haven't we?"

"That's right, Brad," she replied. "We have changed — both of us." Brenda felt an ache inside her as she went on. "That's why you and I getting together again won't solve your problems."

Brad looked away. "I just feel inside that, somehow, we should be together." He shook his head slowly. "We loved each other so much. It seems like such a waste to let it all go." He looked up at her. "And besides, I need you."

Brenda took him by the hand and said, "No. You don't need me." He started to protest, but she put her finger on his lips to silence him. Her training as a counselor had helped her become more assertive and she said, kindly but firmly, "You're going through a painful time right now and sometimes when we hurt, we turn to what's familiar to make us feel better. But it won't make things better, believe me."

"Is that how you really feel?" he asked in a tight voice.

Brenda nodded. "I'm not the Brenda you knew a long time ago. I now know who I am and where I'm going — for the first time in my life. I can't go back." She touched his cheek with her hand. "Neither can you."

Brad's eyes were getting watery, but Brenda could see by the look in them that deep down he understood what she was saying.

Her own eyes started to mist as she said, "I will always care about you, but only as — "

"A friend." Brad finished her sentence for her, his voice scarcely audible.

Brenda bit her lip and nodded. Then she wrapped her arms around him and hugged him tight. "A lifelong friend."

In that moment, a wistful and tender sadness came over them both. They both knew that a special part of their youth had come to a close. It was as if Brenda and Brad had reviewed all the photos in their scrapbook, then closed the cover and put the album away forever.

The music from the patio outside shifted into to a soft ballad. They sat on the couch, gently holding each other, for a long time.

Chapter
15

Stacy stood on tiptoe at the edge of Rose Hill Park, scanning the thick crowd that had gathered to watch the fireworks. She was searching for a familiar profile, one that she had traced over and over in her mind. She crossed the fingers of both hands, then folded her arms across her chest and whispered, "I hope I'm not too late."

The delicious aroma of popcorn and hot dogs rose up from the booths manned by the Rose Hill Kiwanis Club and other civic organizations. Stacy wove her way through thickets of sticky-fingered children, proudly clutching the strings of their brightly colored balloons, while their parents milled around and chatted with friends. Minature American flags were everywhere, and the old-fashioned Victorian gazebo was patriotically draped with red-white-and-blue-striped bunting. A marine band from Arlington, brass instruments gleaming, was just finishing a rousing version of "The Stars and Stripes Forever."

As the applause died down, there was a screech from the P.A. system and the band's conductor, all crisp and starched in his dress military uniform, announced, "Ladies and gentlemen! Let me direct your attention to the big beautiful Maryland sky above us." He pointed up in the air and the first salvo of fireworks shot high into the air, exploding in a shower of red, gold, and green. Everyone in the park "oohed" in unison as the brilliant sparks spread out across the sky.

Over the noise of the crowd, Stacy recognized Jonathan's voice as he cracked, "Man, that was tubular!" She followed the laughter to a low rise bordering the far side of the gazebo, where the Kennedy crowd had gathered to watch the show. Stacy spotted Jonathan and Lily, lying side by side on their backs on a blanket, pointing up at the sky. Katie Crawford was sitting with Greg nearby, her back leaned up against his chest. Both were raptly watching the aerial display above them. Other couples had placed blankets on the grass around them and were huddled together, whispering and giggling in the dark. Stacy looked from group to group to find Zack, but he was nowhere to be seen.

"Katie!" Stacy cried, dashing quickly over to her friend.

Katie looked up and grinned warmly. "Hey, Stace, you're just in time! We were saving a place for you."

"I can't stay," Stacy said breathlessly. "Listen, have you seen Zack tonight?"

Katie shook her head, then tapped Greg on the leg. "Have you seen him, Greg?"

"He's around here somewhere," Greg replied. "Why? What's up?"

Stacy shook her head and said, "I can't explain now. I just *have* to talk to him."

She turned and started to edge around the group, looking anxiously for a glimpse of him in the crowd. Forcing herself to be thorough, Stacy worked her way through the park once again, determined not to overlook any place in her search.

Near the Kiwanis booth she came upon Josh and Frankie, standing in line to get Cokes, and she started to go up to them but stopped. Something in the way they were leaning against each other, oblivious to the world around them, made her ache with envy. Not wanting to disturb them, she pressed back into the swirling crowd.

As she came up beside the picnic tables bordering the duck pond, her heart leaped up in her throat. A lanky blond-haired boy was sitting on top of one of the tables, his back to her. Stacy smiled happily. There weren't too many guys around who had broad muscular shoulders like Zack. It had to be him! She hurried up beside him, then hesitated.

"Zack?" she called shyly, hoping against hope she'd found him.

The boy turned around, and her spirits plummeted back to earth. It wasn't Zack at all. A man sporting a thick blond beard looked up at her inquisitively. "Can I help you?" he said.

Stacy shook her head and stammered, "Oh, I

— I'm sorry! I thought you were someone else!"

Stacy turned away quickly, trying hard to keep from crying. She walked blindly through the crowd, not noticing the jostling and shoving around her.

An especially large firework exploded overhead, the huge boom startling her out of her daze. In the harsh light, she spotted a forlorn figure illuminated against the dark sky. His hands were jammed in his pockets and he was leaning with one leg braced against a tree. Her heart fluttered madly in her chest and she had to force herself not to run over to him. Very carefully, Stacy picked her way around the outskirts of the group and came up beside the boy she was looking for.

Stacy couldn't tell if Zack had noticed she was there or not, and suddenly she found herself speechless with fear. Just standing next to him made her knees feel wobbly but finally, Stacy willed herself to speak.

"Zack?"

He didn't move and Stacy forced herself to continue.

"I — I want to apologize for this morning."

Zack kept his head tilted toward the sky, as if he hadn't heard her at all, and for a second Stacy felt like turning and running. It took all the courage she could muster to go on.

"I know it looked like I was flirting with Brad. Maybe I was, I don't know. I do dumb things sometimes. . . ."

Her throat felt painfully tight and dry. She paused and swallowed hard.

"But that was only because I don't care about him. You have to believe me. Please!"

He didn't respond. Stacy stared at his handsome profile, etched against the sky, and the realization that she might have lost him forever filled her with a terrible, empty ache inside.

"You're the first boy I've ever really cared about," she said, her voice shaking. "Oh, Zack, I'd hate to think that one stupid mistake would ruin everything for us!"

Zack lowered his head and stared hard down at the ground but remained silent. Stacy's eyes welled with tears and she wiped at them hurriedly with her hand. "I didn't plan to cry," she said with a little hiccup, "but I've never had the guts to tell a boy this before, ever." A sob choked her and she hung her head miserably. "And now you won't even look at me!"

She was crying hard now and almost missed hearing his soft voice in the dark.

"Stacy?"

Zack turned his head slowly and looked at her. To her surprise, his eyes were wet and shiny, too.

"Yes?"

"Stacy," he said huskily, "I acted like an impulsive jerk this morning."

"No, you didn't," she barely whispered.

He shook his head and smiled sadly. "I don't know why we make it so hard for each other."

"I don't either," Stacy confessed.

He took hold of her hand and gently pulled her around to face him. Then, his voice shaking with emotion, he said, "I'm really glad you came here tonight!"

Another barrage of rockets exploded overhead, casting gaily colored shadows over their faces. Stacy folded herself into Zack's strong arms and as his lips found hers, she let herself become completely and totally lost in the deliciousness of his kiss.

On the other side of the park, a slender figure in a white dress darted out from the gazebo and moved swiftly to join a dark-haired young man kneeling by himself in the grass.

"Vince?" Roxanne whispered, reaching out and touching his shoulder.

Vince sprang to his feet as if he'd been stung. His eyes were blazing with anger and hurt as he said tersely, "I have nothing to say to you."

"Wait!" she pleaded, reaching her hands out to him. "Just listen, for a minute."

"I've already heard more than I cared to," he said bitterly.

For the first time in her life, Roxanne felt that she didn't need to lie, that the truth was the only way back into Vince's heart. She took a deep breath and confessed, "What Frankie said may have been true once but, I promise you, it's not true anymore!"

Vince turned his back on her, and she stepped in front of him, peering into his dark, soulful eyes. "Vince, please believe me," she begged, "I'm not the same. It's true — I *am* different now. And it's all because of you. I've never felt like this about any boy before. You must have felt it, too, today when we — "

"Don't mention today to me again!" he snapped

at her fiercely, his nostrils flaring with anger. "Ever!"

Roxanne felt as if she had been stripped of all her defenses. She stood before him and said simply, "Vince, I love you!"

Her fervent words hung in the air for a moment, then were drowned out in the noise from the sky above.

"Everyone warned me about you," he said in a dull, lifeless voice. "But I wouldn't listen. No, I told them you had changed." He stared at her with a look of icy hatred. "I feel sick that I let you manipulate me, but much worse, I let my family be poisoned by you, too."

"Don't say that about your family," Roxanne pleaded. "It's not true! It isn't!" She grasped at his sleeve desperately and, in a violent gesture, he shook off her hand.

"I'm through with you," he hissed. "Once and for all." Then Vince spun on his heel and stalked off past the gazebo into the darkness.

A dazzling red, white, and blue firework exploded suddenly overhead, and the crowd burst into applause. A terrible feeling of hopelessness swept over her. Roxanne could feel it in every fiber of her body, as if a heavy hand had gripped her heart. Her legs felt wooden and clumsy as she moved stiffly through the blankets of people toward the edge of the park.

"Roxanne!"

A vaguely familiar voice called out to her, and she looked around to see who it was. Finally her eyes focused on a couple who were seated on the little rise, not five feet away.

"Hey, Rox," Pamela called again, patting a spot beside her. "We've got room on our blanket. Why don't you come and join us?"

"Yeah," Eric echoed beside her, reaching behind him into a red-and-white cooler. "I think there may even be a soda in here with your name on it."

"Thanks, guys." Almost in a daze, Roxanne moved over to sit down beside them.

"After the fireworks, Rox," Molly called from her blanket a few feet away, "I'm serving chicken sandwiches al fresco at our blanket. You're welcome to join us."

Roxanne answered Molly's offer with a grateful smile. She took a sip from the Diet Coke that Eric had handed her and looked around. The irony of it all was overwhelming. If her heart hadn't been breaking, she would have laughed out loud. She had schemed and connived so diligently for so long to get back in the group, and now she had finally won. The crowd had accepted her back. But the joke was on her.

The sky erupted into a stunning panorama of light and sound, forming a giant American flag for the grand finale. The band struck up another rousing march, and everyone in the park started clapping along in time.

Roxanne tilted her head back, fighting the urge to sob, and forced herself to smile bravely up at the sky. Yes, she had won — but without Vince, her victory meant nothing.

Coming soon . . .
Couples #34
DON'T GET CLOSE

Lin looked up from the compass. "Where'd the others go?" she asked Daniel.

"They went to check out that path," Daniel told her, showing her on the map.

"That's no good," Lin said. "It runs straight into that gully. Why did they go there?"

"Because I told them to."

She looked at him curiously. "Why did you tell them to do that?"

"Because I wanted to be alone with you."

Lin didn't looked alarmed. Her gaze was steady and direct. And then it just seemed to happen naturally. He held out his arms, and she folded into them. It was magic; having her in his arms was better than anything he could have ever imagined.

"I'm crazy about you," Daniel whispered. When she didn't respond immediately, he held her tighter. "Lin?"

Her voice was muffled, but he didn't miss a word. "I'm crazy about you, too."

His heart soared. For the next few minutes, they stood there, frozen, clinging together. Then Lin broke free.

"Why did you do that?" Daniel asked, alarmed.

Lin shook her head. "It's . . . it's happening too fast. We have to take it slower."

"Why?"

"Because that's the way I am." Her eyes implored him to understand. "I don't like to get into things too fast, Daniel."

"But you do care for me, don't you?"

Her eyes were soft. "Isn't that obvious?"

"Then why hold back?" Daniel asked urgently. "We both feel the same way. It's right, I can feel it."

"I'm sorry," Lin said simply. "It's the way I am."

For a moment, she stared at the ground. Then, almost unwillingly, she looked up. Their eyes locked. Almost reluctantly, as if it were against her will, she opened her arms to him.

And then they were holding each other again, as tightly as they could.